Acclaim for **Jay McInerney**'s
Model Behavior

"*Model Behavior* is very funny, and full of the rakish, old-fashioned literary elegance that McInerney always manages to mix into the slangy idioms of his characters."
— *The New York Review of Books*

"McInerney has emerged as an uncommonly resourceful, if not always compelling, novelist and social critic."
— *Chicago Tribune*

"Entertaining." — *The Wall Street Journal*

"Smart, funny, sexy and well observed." — *Esquire*

"McInerney is the real thing, a writer of undeniable flair and charm." — *Entertainment Weekly*

"Like *Bright Lights, Model Behavior* is a quintessentially New York story. And like the city itself, McInerney's latest is bound to chafe in places. But no one who truly loves Manhattan in all its soiled beauty and shopworn glamour can fail to derive pleasure from this book." — *New York Post*

"Facile and funny. . . . McInerney's observations . . . never fail to entertain." — *The Plain Dealer*

"Jay McInerney has developed into one of the sharpest social observers writing contemporary fiction." — *The Seattle Times*

"McInerney is unquestionably a sharp observer of society and its mores."
                                                    —*Time Out New York*

"High comedy and low living. . . . A frighteningly evocative idea of the temptations of indulging an addictive, self-observed personality. . . . McInerney demonstrates compassion as well as contempt for these spectacularly dysfunctional figures."
                                    —*Times Literary Supplement* (London)

"Entertaining. . . . McInerney's wit and wordplay work overtime."
                                                    —*The Hartford Courant*

"McInerney writes with great wit and verbal ingenuity." —*Salon*

"*Model Behavior* does for the nineties what *Bright Lights, Big City* did for the eighties. It is just as stylish, just as sharp, not quite as sad; if anything, funnier."
                                    —*The Independent on Sunday* (London)

"*Model Behavior* is clever and witty. . . . It makes a very insightful comment on society's celebrity worship."
                                                    —*Richmond Times-Dispatch*

"Funny. . . . McInerney can still turn a phrase."
                                                    —*Rocky Mountain News*

"An affecting examination of the ways and means of our celeb-obsessed culture."
                                                    —*Gear*

"Lines that drip with wit and scenes that percolate with hilarity. McInerney is most powerful when he writes of things that both attract and repel him. . . . His magic is that he is a writer who continues to experiment."   —*St. Petersburg Times*

Jay McInerney
Model Behavior

Jay McInerney lives with his wife and their two children in New York and Williamson County, Tennessee.

Model Behavior

Model Behavior

a novel

Jay McInerney

VINTAGE CONTEMPORARIES
Vintage Books
A Division of Random House, Inc.
New York

The Library of Congress has cataloged the Knopf edition as follows:
McInerney, Jay.
Model behavior : a novel and stories / Jay McInerney. — 1st ed.
p. cm.
ISBN 0-679-42846-1
1. United States—Social life and customs—20th century—Fiction.
I. Title.
PS3563.C3694M6 1998
813'54—dc21 98-27859
CIP

Vintage ISBN: 0-679-74953-5

Author photograph © Dan Borris

www.vintagebooks.com

Printed in the United States of America
10 9 8 7 6 5 4 3 2 1

For Scott Sommer

Model Behavior

MODEL COUPLE

When Philomena looks in the mirror she sees a creature fat and unattractive. This despite the fact that she is a woman whose photographic image is expensively employed to arouse desire in conjunction with certain consumer goods. Or rather, *because* of that fact. Toxic body consciousness being the black lung of her profession. Dressing for the party, she screams that she's bloated and has nothing to wear.

I'm clutching a preparty martini when she makes this declaration. "You look terrific," I say.

She seizes my glass and hurls it at the mirror, shattering both.

It's all right, really. I drink too much anyway.

THE PARTY

The name of the party is the Party You Have Been to Six Hundred Times Already. Everybody is here. "All your friends," Philomena states in what can only be described as a citric tone. It seems to me that they are *her* friends, that *she* is the reason we grace this fabulous gala, which takes place in the Waiting Room of Grand Central, presumably evicting dozens of homeless people for the night. We're supposedly on hand for the benefit of a disease, but we were comped, as was everyone else we know. "I'm sick of all this pointless glamour," my glamorous girlfriend says. "I want the simple life." This has become a theme. Weariness with metropolitan life in all its colonoscopic intricacy. I wonder if this ennui is somehow related to that other unstated domestic theme: sex, infrequency thereof.

We are accosted by Belinda, the popular transvestite, whom I am nearly certain is a friend of my girlfriend's, as opposed to one of my very own. I can't exactly remember if I know him from the gossip columns or if I know him personally, from events like these. Belinda is with an actual, ageless woman with striking dark eyebrows and buzzcut white hair, a woman who is always here at the party and whom I always sort of recognize. One of those women with three names: Hi Howareyou Goodtoseeyou. All the women lately have either three names or just one. Even the impersonators.

"Oh God, hide me," says the woman whose name I always forget, "there's Tommy Kroger, I had a bad date with him about five thousand years ago."

"Did you sleep with him?" Philomena asks, raising one of her perfectly defined eyebrows, which looks like a crow in flight in the far distance of a painting by van Gogh.

"God, who can remember?"

"If you can't, then you did," says Belinda. "That's the rule."

Ah, so *that's* the rule.

"Hello, darlings." Who could it be but Delia McFaggen, the famous designer, streaking toward Belinda, blowing kisses all over everyone. I retreat, slaloming through the thick crowd to find beverages, the first of many trips.

A FRIENDLY FACE

At the bar I encounter Jeremy Green, an unlikely and conspicuous figure at this venue, his golden locks falling superabundantly across the square shoulders of his rented tux—which juxtaposition suggests a flock of begowned angels camped atop the Seagram Building. He is an actual friend, my best friend, in fact, though he ignores my repeated greetings. Not until I pour vodka on his shirt does he deign to acknowledge my existence.

"Fuck off."

"Excuse me. Aren't you Jeremy Green, the famous short story writer?"

"That's an oxymoron. Same category as *living poet, French rock star, German cuisine.*"

"How about Chekhov?"

"Dead." Jeremy pronounces this verdict with a poète maudit manner that seems tinged more than faintly with envy. He doesn't quite add *Lucky bastard*, but you can see that's what he's thinking.

"Carver?"

"Ditto. Plus, you think the guy who read his gas meter knew who Carver was? You think this bartender knows?"

The bartender, an aspiring model, says "*Shortcuts*" in midpour.

"I saw the movie."

"I think," Jeremy says, "that proves my point. And don't even think about saying *Hemingway*."

"Wouldn't dream of it. Any particular reason you're ignoring me?"

"I just think I'll feel better about myself if I pretend I don't know anybody at this hideous ratfuck." Finally he turns his wrathful gaze upon me. "Besides, if memory serves, you're the slimy lowlife who talked me into attending this fetid fete."

"Your *editor* talked you into it," I remind him. "I merely encouraged you by way of saying that *I*, personally, would be happier and less chagrined if you were among the throng."

Why, I wonder, are all the boys and girls blaming *me* tonight? Jeremy has a book coming out, and his editor, Blaine Forrestal, thought it would be good for him to be seen. Blaine is part of this world. She wears terrific suits, has a Radcliffe degree and a house in Sag Harbor; Jeremy is the least commercial of the writers she publishes. In fact, one might surmise that she is publishing Jeremy as a kind of penance for the frothy, wildly successful stuff she generally dispenses—memoirs by disgraced politicians, autobiographies by Emmy-winning TV stars. Jeremy's stories tend to appear in *Antaeus* and the *Iowa Review* and frequently are set in mental institutions.

"I feel," he says, "like a whore."

"Now you know how the rest of us feel."

"I'm sure this will really boost my lit cred, showing all the media elite that I swim in the same sewer they do."

"Don't worry, I think the media elite's swimming in some other sewer tonight." Indeed, excepting a few young black-clad Voguettes and self, I don't see much in the way of the Fourth Estate.

"Who's that fucking midget over there who told me he 'rather liked' my first book."

Following Jeremy's aquiline nose, I spot Kevin Shipley, book assassin for *Beau Monde*, in conversation with the *New York Post*.

"Jesus, I hope you didn't insult him. That's Kevin Shipley."

"He told me he bought it on the remainder table at Barnes and Noble and I said I was deeply honored that he felt he'd gotten his buck ninety-five's worth."

"Just pray he doesn't review the new one. His keyboard's made out of human teeth."

"Yeah, but how does he reach it?"

Finally I have reached the bar, where I request several cosmopolitans, one of which I hand to Jeremy. "Your problem," I say, "is that you don't drink enough. Where's Blaine, anyway?"

"Last I knew she was kissing Hollywood butt. Some fucking troll from Sony Pictures."

"Let's go find Phil," I suggest. "Maybe you can cheer her up."

WHAT'S WITH PHILOMENA?

The love of my life has been decidedly edgy and nervous. I would ask her why, except I'm not entirely certain I want to know. What we need is some ecstasy therapy, drop a few tabs, have a long night of truth and touch. There has been too little rapture of late. Not to mention the touching part.

Fortunately, by the time I find her again, she seems to have undergone a mood transplant. Delighted to see Jeremy, she kisses him and then, for good measure, me.

I introduce myself to the attractive young woman of color with whom Phil has been conversing, whose name sounds familiar.

"Do I know you?" I ask.

"We've never met," she says. "I'm Chip Ralston's personal assistant."

"Well," says Jeremy, "bully for you."

"I was just telling Cherie," Phil tells me, "that you're doing the profile for *CiaoBella!*"

A photographer suddenly appears: "Philomena, let's get a shot."

My statuesque soulmate breaks into autosmile and gamely reaches for my arm, but, shy guy that I am, I say, "Do a shot with Jeremy, we're trying to get him noticed." Shoving them together, I chase after the retreating personal assistant.

"Is Chip *here*," I ask.

"You just missed him," she says. "He's flying back to L.A. tonight, but I gave him your message. I'm sure he'll check in with you next week."

I'd press her harder, I've got to talk to the bastard, but soon, then I suddenly see that she's edging directly into the path of Jillian Crowe, my formidably glamorous boss; and while I admire Jillian's fashion sense and editorial skills, I'd just as soon avoid her at present. Backtracking, I find Philomena teasing Jeremy about the career that awaits him in modeling. She is more vivacious than I've seen her in days, Jeremy being such a Jeremiah that he tends to spur his companions to sparkle and shine.

Fueled by several uncharacteristic cocktails, Philomena's high spirits last well into the morning; she surprises me by agreeing to join an expedition of fashion folk down to the Baby Doll Lounge, a low strip joint in TriBeCa.

Cabbing down with three revelers—satellites of Planet Fashion—she sits on my lap and sips from a drink she managed to smuggle out of the party. "I have a joke," she suddenly announces.

TOPLESS MODEL IN HEADLESS BAR

At the Baby Doll, Philomena orders another cosmopolitan and, not unkindly, critiques the bodies of the dancing girls. With the body God gave Phil, she can afford to be generous. Finally the guy named Ralph, whom Philomena introduced as "genius with hair," suggests that Philomena show us her tits. The cry is taken up by

Alonzo—who introduced himself as "a powder fairy," which Philomena annotated as "makeup guy"—and then by the adjoining tables. To my astonishment, she jumps on the bar and pulls her dress down to her waist, giving us a liberal flash of lunar breast. And it is a measure of their excellence of form that I nearly swoon—if indeed one can *nearly* swoon—despite having seen them nearly every day for the past three years of my life. Tumid with desire, I try to coax Philomena home the minute she jumps down from the bar. But she's on a roll. Wants to dance. Wants another cosmopolitan.

For the third time I try the men's room and it's still locked.

SHIPS IN THE NIGHT

We continue to have an uproarious time, but by now I have lost the feeling of being in the moment, and stand as if on the sidelines watching Philomena entertain her friends, though I dance and drink with the best of them. I don't mind, it's good to see her like this. Alonzo, feeling no pain either, slips me his phone number and says we ought to get together sometime. I explain to him that while I appreciate the thought, he is barking up the wrong telephone pole. He raises a skeptical eyebrow, then plants a hand voguishly on his hip. Working as I do for a young women's magazine with a strong emphasis on fashion, I often encounter this suspicion.

Philomena's mood slips away when I'm not looking, possibly around the time that Ralph's giving me his card and telling me that I have to do something about my haircut immediately, for the sake of the nation. "They actually let you into the offices of *CiaoBella!* with that do?"

"Maybe he really *is* straight," says Ralph.

By the time we get in the cab my love is silent and pensive. As we undress for bed, she announces preemptively that she's exhausted.

No nookie for you, buckaroo.

AT LONG LAST, SEX

The narrator, slightly hungover now, the day after the party, helps Philomena choose the outfits for her trip—a versatile taupe suit from Jil Sander, a Versace jacket and ripped jeans for the plane, a fetching little sheath from Nicole Miller for the audition, as well as an extra pair of ripped, faded jeans plus three immaculate white T-shirts. And some nice clunky boots suitable for heavy construction or light shopping in SoHo. If he were more attentive it's possible the narrator would pick up certain clues from the packing, or from her behavior, indications that this trip might be something more than advertised, but he is not a suspicious person by nature, and his powers of observation are swamped by a surge of hormones. When, after trying on the sheath, she slips out of it and asks him to fetch some panties from her dainties drawer, he is overcome with desire for the taut, tawny flesh beneath her teddy.

"Please," he pleads. "Just a little slice." He reminds her that it has been five days, nine hours, and thirty-six minutes. And they're not even married yet.

"No we're not, are we?" Oh, dear, a tactical mistake on his part, this allusion to matrimony. This is a sore point, something he has been meaning to get around to addressing for the last couple of years. While she has been waiting for the big question, he is waiting to be worthy of such an honor; he does not believe that anyone, let alone Philomena, could really want to hitch her shining carriage to his lame gelding. Yet for some reason she seems to want to do so. As long as he is only a boyfriend, he believes that his fortunes are still fluid, that his lowly station is merely a stage of gestation. Whereas she believes that the actual obstacle is his sense of superiority. Luckily she doesn't pursue the subject, though perhaps with the absence of a marriage proposal in mind she makes him kneel and beg for it.

Craven, genuflective begging ensues, as per standard form. But heartfelt and genuine on his part. PLEASE PLEASE PLEASE. Feeling like the target audience for the recent beer commercial in which she appeared, oiled and glistening in a bikini, he tells her he will do anything. He will bark like any species of canine she can name and, if necessary, roll over. Finally she peels off the teddy and lies back on the bed like Manet's *Olympia*, ripe and haughty, a bored odalisque.

"Fast," she commands, "and no sweating."

The narrator takes what he can get, a grateful consumer.

AFTERGLOW

Afterward, lying in bed, a single gemlike tear appears on Philomena's cheek. When I ask what's wrong, she concocts a smile and shakes her head.

"Don't worry," I say, although I have no idea what I mean by this hollow formula. While I am full of doubt as to the future, my job, I feel, is to reassure her, my consort, my lost little girl.

Later, a moment of perfect melancholy: watching Philomena gather her cosmetics at her vanity in front of the cracked mirror, the dusky dimness infiltrated with pulsing red light that strobes through the window slats of our half-basement bedroom. This lurid glow likely signifying a more permanent death than the one I have just experienced; across the street is a nursing home where ambulances call with some regularity.

"Don't go," I say in a sudden swoon of dread.

"It's just for a few days," she says, brushing her hair.

"I love you," I say—a too-rare declaration.

She smiles at me from a shard of mirror.

LOCATION, LOCATION, LOCATION

We live in the West Village, near the river, on the southern edge of the Meat District, far enough west that we are largely spared the Visigoth invasions of provincial teens with boom boxes. Of a summer's evening the breeze is frequently infused with the stench of decaying flesh wafting from the scrap heaps of the warehouses; after dark, the streets outside the butcheries are taken over by transvestites and the cruising vehicles of their johns; many nights we will be awakened by thick whispers and carnal grunts from the stairwell just outside the bedroom windows. Love and death. "It's always a trade-off with Manhattan real estate," our agent cheerfully informed us, just before she demanded seventeen percent of our first year's rent.

POSTCOITAL REFLECTIONS

Meditating on the strange fact that while you were making love to Philomena you were actually fantasizing about a previous fucking. With Philomena—so she has no real grounds for complaint, though even so you don't propose to share this insight. This has become almost a habit, conjuring a previous sexual episode in the commission of a current one, as if the memory possessed a vivacity somehow lacking in the physical present. As if, say, the breast of Philomena, delectable as it might seem in the flesh, was only truly eroticized in the imagination. But why isn't the flesh enough?

You have a repertoire of sexual memories, and in time this latest act might be added to it, but while happening it was experienced through the scrim of a recycled midsummer encounter behind a beach house in Amagansett. Sex itself becoming, according to this model, merely the raw material for an aesthetic event.

IMMEDIATE FAMILY

My sister, Brooke, has a tiny rent-controlled apartment in the Geritol Zone off Beekman Place. Not long after putting Philomena in a car for the airport I call, but she will not pick up her phone. I know she's there, listening to the messages. I know because I am my sister's keeper. Maybe it's my hangover, or perhaps the ambulance has made me jumpy and morbid; nonetheless I'm filled with a sense of the fragility of life, love and the social contract. That something bad is about to happen feels as palpable as rain in the air. I consider calling the airline, to see if Phil's plane is okay. Except come to think of it, I don't know which airline, which flight.

Instead I walk out to Hudson beneath the yellowing stingko trees. Wait for a cab, sharing the sidewalk with nocturnal pigeons who waddle uptown like portly tourists.

At the door of Brooke's building, trying to flush her out of her lair, which takes longer than the cab ride uptown. Finally the intercom crackles to life. She beams me up after I identify myself as her only sibling. Pushing through the cracked door, I find her in bed, reading, bones poking through the sheets, her beautiful strawberry-blond hair unwashed. When I kiss her, her breath has the hollow keloid stench of starvation, of the body consuming itself. I try not to look alarmed.

"They made separate piles of the body parts," she says in greeting. "Legs in one pile, arms in another. Living torsos on a pile of other torsos six feet high. Their neighbors. People they had lived with for years."

"Bosnia?"

"Rwanda."

Brooke is reading transcripts from the UN War Crimes Tribunal. On the headboard of her sleigh bed she has taped a map of the former Yugoslavia. Sarajevo, Mostar, Srebrenica and other unfortunate cities are circled in red ink. Lately she has taken up the study of the recent atrocities in Central Africa.

Searching the kitchen cupboards, I discover an inch of Orville Redenbacher's popcorn in the bottom of a jar and a half inch of olive oil in another. I fire up a bowl, bring it back to the bedroom, casually placing it within reach of her delicate, freckled hand on the bed.

"How's Mad Dog," I ask, this being my ironic appellation for Doug Halliwell, M.D., her current would-be consort. Doug is a trauma surgeon whose acquaintance Brooke made in the ER at New York Hospital after she tumbled down a set of stairs at Rockefeller University. To me he does not seem worthy of my sister's attention, let alone any of her now-mended body parts. Not that I really imagine Doug has actually gotten hold of any of them just yet. Brooke's on the rebound from a colorful marriage, hence this sudden tolerance for beige.

"I wish you'd stop calling him that. Doug's fine. And how's the mannequin? Has she mastered the alphabet yet?"

"She's in San Francisco on a shoot," I say. "And for your information she took *Anna Karenina* on the plane."

"You enjoy saying that don't you? *On a shoot. On location.* The jargon of the glamour industry."

"Well, let's just say she's on a business trip."

"Do you know that one of the reasons the Hutus hated the Tutsis is because the Tutsis were considered more attractive? Tall, thin noses, lighter skin."

"Are you suggesting that the secretaries at Ford and Click might rise up and kill all the models?"

"Seems like she's been traveling a lot lately."

"Why wouldn't she?"

"Hmmmm," she hums.

Brooke is not a fan of Philomena's. And vice versa. Phil calls Brooke the scrambled egghead. Which goes to show that she's far sharper than Brooke would ever concede. Staying loyal to both has been difficult. While I'm used to Brooke's skepticism vis-à-vis my squeeze, tonight it makes me anxious. My ribs shrink around my lungs. What does Brooke know that I don't?

Why do I always feel that everyone has more information than me? Actually, Brooke knows a great deal that I don't know: the difference between natural and unnatural numbers, the significance of Heisenberg's indeterminacy principle, Gödel's incompleteness theorem, the probable casualties from Banja Luka and environs. Until recently Brooke was doing postgraduate work in physics at Rockefeller University, but she is on an extended hiatus, crippled by depression and an acute sensitivity to human suffering. My sister resembles one of those bubble children who are born without an immune system; she does not possess that protective membrane that filters out the noise and pain of other creatures. She is utterly porous.

Mom and Dad think it has to do with witnessing a murder at age seven. And while that would be enough to fuck most of us up, Brooke decidedly is not most of us.

"So how was *your* day?" I ask, fishing. *Something* must have gone wrong, whether on a global or personal level.

"My day? Well, let's see . . . it started with Jerry on the *Today Show* explaining the proton accelerator to a grateful nation."

Ah, yes. Here's the pea under the mattress, the fly in the K-Y. Until recently Brooke was married to a prodigious young Harvard professor, Jerry Sakoloff, who wrote an improbable best-seller about quantum physics and who frequently appears on television to explain subatomic phenomena. Brooke had been Jerry's student when their romance commenced; the problem was that Jerry continued to sleep with other students after he and Brooke were married. Or rather, the problem was that he didn't at all see why he shouldn't and in fact insisted on bringing them home to befriend his wife. It's hard to say which upset Brooke more, the infidelity or the television appearances.

"How was he?"

"Charming. Quotable. Hair and tie askew for that authentic, absentminded professorial look. Before those shows he'd work on the tie for twenty minutes so the knot would hang just low enough that it looked like he'd forgotten to pull it up all the way. And brush his hair within an inch of its life, then muss it up with his fingers — you know, as if he'd been tearing at it while pondering the great problems of the universe."

"If I'd been here instead of Japan I never would've let you marry him."

"You wouldn't have let me marry anybody."

"I do think you might consider the life of a nun. Lord knows, the Church could certainly use you." This an allusion to the discarded but indelible faith of our forefathers.

I pretend to look aimlessly around the room while attempting to will her to eat the popcorn. EAT EAT EAT EAT.

"How are the beautiful people," she asks, reaching down and tweezing a kernel of popcorn between thumb and forefinger.

"They're fabulous, by definition," I answer, watching out of the corner of my eye as she inserts the popped kernel between her lips. CHEW CHEW SWALLOW SWALLOW.

"What about that young actor who died? The one with the weird hippie name." Her hand is in the bowl again, and she's actually chewing! "Did you know him?"

"You mean River Phoenix? Brooke, that was, like, years ago. This is 1996."

"So, excuse me, I'm not a big maven of popular culture."

"Okay, so I spent a few hours with him at the Olive, which was this club in West Hollywood, when I was doing a piece on his girlfriend. Let's just say it's a wonder he lasted as long as he did."

LISTEN TO YOURSELF

Lord, listen to you. How embarrassing that you even know this shit. How pathetic, the offhand manner in which you exhale this little toxic cloud of inside dope.

Meanwhile you are worrying that Philomena *does* seem to be taking a lot of trips lately. And why wouldn't she know where she was staying? Or if she did know, why wouldn't she leave you her number?

But hey, wait a minute—this is ridiculous. You trust her. Right? Well, yes, basically, although you can't quite ignore the merest tingle of suspicion, of dread, that animates the hairs at the base of your neck.

ANOREXIA STRIKES DEEP

Once Brooke is fully engaged with the popcorn I repair to the kitchen to warm a can of Campbell's chicken noodle soup. "*Um-um good,*" I call out. "Just like Mom used to heat." No, actually, come to think of it, Mom would ask the housekeeper, Daisy, to do the heavy lifting. Anyway. I pour the nourishing liquid into a big Harvard mug and carry it in on a plastic tray, treading cautiously so as not to frighten the prey. In her approach to eating my sister is rather like a stray dog we adopted as children who was so used to stealing food that he couldn't eat while anyone was looking. Any direct reference to nutrition will scare her off for days. Neither, of course, are we allowed to speak the name of her illness. Several years ago, at the nadir of her emaciation, she told me that the average weight loss among adult residents of Sarajevo after a thousand days of siege was twenty-five pounds, thereby giving her fast a symbolic dimension, but the siege is long over, and anyway she's been starving herself on and off since the Vietnam War.

Toward the end of her marriage to Jerry she began to cut herself—small, razored incisions on her arms and legs.

IMMEDIATE FOREBEARS

"Talked to the 'rents lately?" I ask. Although not actually eating the soup, Brooke is blowing at it, a hopeful sign.

"Dad called a few days ago," Brooke says.

"How was that?"

"I find it strangely reassuring—the sound of ice cubes against glass."

"Crystal," I correct.

"You have to give them credit, though—our parents—for being the only couple in America still together after forty-odd years."

"Indeed." Our father inherited orange groves in Central Florida from his father, who at the age of fifty sold his seat on the New York Stock Exchange and followed the sun. The property produces just enough income to keep my father in bourbon, Brooks Brothers shirts and Book-of-the-Month Club Main Selections for life. Exactly enough to kill any ambition he might have had to actually work for a living. Not enough that there will be anything left for us after estate taxes. Every few years Dad sells off five acres to finance a trip to Europe. So don't worry about a looming inheritance spoiling me. Dad reads the classics—Grisham, Clancy and Crichton—plays tennis and keeps a fond paternal eye on the oranges. Mom reads poetry, paints landscapes and sips her drinkie. Cummings is her favorite poet, Bonnard her painterly hero, Pernod her current preferred tipple.

Oranges are not exactly labor-intensive. They grow while you sleep, while you drink, while you play tennis, while you paint, while you nap. And they are still growing when you wake up to stir another cocktail. Twice a year the migrant laborers come to pick them, and sometimes a frost blowing down from the North will necessitate the application of smudge pots and extra-strength cocktails. Conveniently, oranges are monoecious, containing both sex organs in the same blossom—the laziest of fruit.

Unlike Brooke my parents don't worry enough. The worry muscles are thoroughly atrophied. Every fall they spend a week in New York. In just a few days, they will arrive to celebrate Thanksgiving with us here in the city. Gobble gobble gobble.

"How can people live together for years and suddenly start to butcher their neighbors," Brooke asks. "What happens to them? Is there a fucking light switch on the moral faculty?"

"Are we talking Rwanda here?"

"*That's* what's so depressing. The situation was identical in both places."

Devoid of insight, I hold the mug to her lips, tilting it toward her. One tries to distract her from these idées fixes, even at the best of times. When my sister isn't depressed, she talks about Boolean binary lattices and icosahedral symmetries with an enthusiasm that calls for a gag order.

My sister, my beautiful tomboy sibling with an IQ like the surface temperature of the planet Venus.

MOUNT OLYMPUS

I slip away while Brooke is watching a special war crimes edition of *Nightline*, stopping at a cash machine to draw out two hundred dollars, which leaves a residue of three hundred seventy-one dollars and change. Must get a draw from the magazine. From the street I decide to call Jeremy as a possible accomplice for whatever comes next. The message on his machine says: "Hi, I'm either out or I'm sitting here listening to see who you are before I pick up. So if you're willing to risk rejection, go ahead and leave a message after the beep."

I identify myself as a member of the committee distributing the

MacArthur genius awards. "If you pick up within the next ten seconds you will receive a grant of sixty thousand tax-free dollars a year for five years in recognition of your services to literature, but only if you answer the phone immediately."

What does it mean when your friends and relatives won't take your calls?

Thus, a cab to Mount Olympus, where, at least, the tuxedoed doorgent appears delighted to see me. "How are *you*, sir?" His bonhomie is such that I feel obliged to give him five dollars on top of the fifteen for admission.

I enter a universe of twinned spheres, silicone heaven. In ancient times, you may recall, blocks of marble were cleaved from the earth in the vicinity of Carrara and coaxed into the likeness of deities; now it is living flesh which is sculpted into goddess form at the hands of surgeons and personal trainers. Look, there's Cassandra, of the wine-dark hair, dancing nipples to nose with a baldie. And Demeter, shaking her booty for three mesmerized Japanese businessmen. *Kirei, desu ne?* But where is my own personal goddess, the celestial Pallas? A hostess in white garters with whom I am unacquainted greets me and brings me to a table. Squeezing past the Japanese businessmen—oops, bumping *into* the Japanese businessman, who spills his drink all over his navy-blue suit. *Domo summimasen.*

At last I spot her, three tables away, table dancing for an aging mortal in a chalk-striped suit. From this distance his skin appears scaly, beneath patchy tufts of hair, and I am nearly certain he has horns. I watch in horror as Pallas shimmies closer and closer, her rare, all-natural breasts dipping within inches of the foul creature. Suddenly my view is eclipsed by a field of blue sequins. "Hi, I'm Isis. Would you like a dance?" She is very pretty, a light brown woman with long, straight obsidian hair—not cornrows, as you might expect in a fertility goddess. It makes me feel bad that I have to turn her down, though I know she makes about a thousand dollars a night and is unlikely to take it personally. That is the principle at work here: to make it *seem* personal. How could you say no to a beautiful girl who wants to dance naked for you and you alone? A fairly effective principle all in all. But if I fail to conserve my funds, at twenty a dance, I could be busted in ten minutes, and I am sworn to wait for the divine Pallas. Whatever happened to "Ten Cents a Dance"?

The hostess relieves me of my credit card. Thanks, that was getting heavy in my pocket. Low on cash or no, I would still give a hundred bucks if someone would promise to destroy every single recorded copy of Rod Stewart's "Do Ya Think I'm Sexy?" which is now playing, animating some dozen pelvi and two dozen pendant glands in parabolas of simulated seduction.

Watching the other men. Sorry bastards. In groups they are emboldened, leering and winking at each other, tossing their horned heads with exaggerated nonchalance, but the singles are as shy and solemn as Japanese rock fans, not quite sure what to do with their hands or facial muscles. They look, in a word, ridiculous. And I am one of them. Sitting at our tables naked with yearning, inappropriately dressed for the party. We are penises trussed up in wool suits and silk ties. Blind voyeurs, we dimly suspect that the joke is on us. Can you imagine how they talk about us, the dancers? Thank God our drink has arrived. We gulp half of it before it touches the table. Another dancer shimmies up. "Hi, I'm Dawn, what's your name?"

CURRICULUM VITAE

The narrator's name is Connor McKnight. That's me. Hello. Connor here. Thirty-two and two-thirds years old and not really happy about it. Still waiting for his adult life to begin. Is this *his* fault, or *life's* fault? He could blame his parents, perhaps; that would be novel. Or perhaps the real problem was the seven years he spent in Japan. First in Kyoto studying Japanese literature, a large and highly speculative investment of time whose dubious value plummeted the moment he decided to stop short of his Ph.D. Then in a Zen monastery in Kamakura, counting his breaths.

I do think I missed something while turning Japanese. In fact, that was what brought me back, the suspicion that I was missing something back here. Still waiting to find out what it was, exactly. Not Rod Stewart's "Do Ya Think I'm Sexy?"—nope, that was practically the fucking soundtrack of my sojourn in Nippon, playing in the hidden upstairs "snacks" of Roppongi and the pubs of Shinjuku and the ward office where I renewed my alien registration every six months, an abiding whine like a mosquito in the dark of a musty summer bedroom or like the tune in a Warner Bros. cartoon which cannot be stilled even after Elmer Fudd or Sylvester the Cat smashes the radio to smithereens with a sledgehammer, demolishes the still-singing speaker tweeter and drops it down a well . . . even then, you can still hear the faint adenoidal bad-hair voice of the Rodster.

I have a job, of sorts. The name of my job is Paying the Rent Until I Write My Original Screenplay About Truth and Beauty. Specifically: writing articles about celebrities for *CiaoBella!*—a lifestyle magazine for young women. Much of the magazine is devoted to telling our readers what to wear and how to snare boyfriends. I am hagiographer to their saints—those men and women who, in simulating real life on large and small screen, are transubstantiated into beings who are far more real than those who watch them.

THE NEW ONTOLOGY

In the new ontology, nothing exists until it has been reproduced on film stock. (Or videotape.)

CONNOR McKNIGHT, ONTOLOGIST

I can't claim that it's hard work, verifying the reality of the new idols, describing their diets and dating rituals. In fact, I'm planning to develop a computer program which will spit these things out with the touch of a few keys, freeing me up to squander even more time than I do now. It would be a simple program, since this genre offers very few variables. Already my word-processing program contains macro keystrokes which instantly call up such phrases as "shuns the Hollywood limelight in favor of spending quality time with his family at his sprawling ranch outside of Livingston, Montana" (CTRL, *Mont*). And: "There's nothing like being a parent to teach you what really matters in life. The fame, the money, the limos—you can keep it. I mean, being a father/mother is more important to me than any movie role could ever be" (ALT, *baby*). And the ever popular "Actually, I've always been really insecure about my looks. I definitely don't think of myself as a sex symbol. When I look in a mirror I'm like—*Oh, God, what a mess*" (SHIFT, *What, me sexy?*). This is pretty basic stuff, though. What's needed is a program employing a spin factor with numerical values from, say, 20 (ax murder) to 1 (blow job, swallow). Journalism by the numbers. For my purposes, and that of most other high-sheen magazines, number one would be the default setting. ("Despite his tough guy image, ——— likes nothing better than a quiet night at home with a volume of poetry.")

I'm always amused when someone asks me about some actor I have interviewed: "What's he really like?" To which the only honest response is "What's he *like*? He's an *actor*, for Christ's sake."

Right now I'm trying to write a profile of Chip Ralston, boy movie star, but I cannot seem to track him down. Although he allegedly agreed to the piece, his agent, his business manager *and* his personal assistant are all behaving somewhat evasively, while his publicist is being an unmitigated bitch. Is it possible he remembers a rather negative—all right, way negative (18.5)—review I wrote a few years back in the *Tokyo Business Journal* about his second movie in which I said the best acting was done by his car, a British racing-green Austin Healy with sexy wire wheels and a deep throaty voice? Scuttlebutt, however, has it that Chip can't read.

When I mentioned the proposed interview to Philomena, she said, "I hear he's kind of a jerk."

To which I responded, "Phil, honey, he's an *actor*."

Forgetting that Philomena is herself an aspiring thespian.

P A L L A S

"Wow, that must be really interesting, getting to meet all those famous people," says Dawn, rosy fingered from handling ice-cold beverages here on the slopes of Mount Olympus.

"Yeah, well," I say. "I'm also writing a book about Akira Kurosawa. The film director," I add helpfully. This is true almost, though at present I'm mired in the early middle of the first chapter.

"We get a lot of Japanese gentlemen here."

At last—I see Pallas gliding toward me, a vision in gold sequins and matching hair. "Hey, Connor." The sound of my name on her lips makes me weak. "Want me to dance for you?" She is so lovely it hurts my teeth to look at her.

"Not yet," I gasp. "Let's have a drink first." I know the rules: she lifts the hem of her long form-fitting one-piece sequin dress up her sinuous calf, over her knee, and I deposit two twenties in her garter, hoping that will hold her for a while.

Pallas sits down beside me. "What do you know?" This is her customary greeting, a locution she seems to have imported from her native Kentucky.

"I know the ending of *The Charterhouse of Parma*," I say, "but I wouldn't want to spoil it for you."

She smiles, impervious to my lame attempt at equalizing the balance of power.

"More properly known as *La Chartreuse de Parme*," I explain, "by Stendhal, not to be confused with *The Porterhouse of Chartres*, a book I might soon write about the role of medieval nutrition in the development of flying buttresses, or with *The Porter of Chartreux*, by Gervaise Latouche, which I commend to you as a very filthy, dirty book indeed."

I always have a different answer, and she always listens and smiles like a doctor in the presence of a colorful but harmless lunatic.

"Come to the theater with me tomorrow," I suggest. "I have tickets to the new Nicky Silver play."

"I'm working," she says. "Is he the guy who does the *Lethal Weapon* movies?"

"Not exactly."

"Chip Ralston was in here a few nights ago," she says, eyes aglow.

"*Chip Ralston?*" Imagine me all agog. "I've been looking for that bastard for two weeks. Are you sure it was Chip Ralston?"

"He was really nice."

"Then it was probably somebody else."

"No, really. He was . . ." She pauses to refine her impressions. "Nice."

"Nice? What's that supposed to mean?"

"He was, you know, like a regular guy."

"*Like* is the operative word in that sentence. Physically he *resembles* a human being—in fact he often plays one—but he's a nasty little shit with lifts in his shoes and a silicone-enhanced ego. You noticed, I hope, that he's shorter than you? He didn't leave his phone number by any chance, did he?"

"What are you so mad about?" Pallas asks. "What did Chip Ralston ever do to you?"

WHERE DO YOU START?

"What did he do to me? Everything. Right off the bat, I'm mad at him because he's making my life difficult by not returning my calls. In the larger scheme, he is sucking up all the fame and money and adulation of women which might, in a more just universe, accrue to a more worthy party. Generally speaking it's not worth liking or disliking movie stars—they're like the weather, for God's sake—but this guy is really beginning to piss me off."

WHAT CHIP IS LIKE

I try to pump her for information, anecdotes, dirt, scandal—anything I could use for my piece. But Pallas is as vague as a bowl of rice. Could she be a secret Buddhist, attuned to the oneness of the many? She keeps repeating that he was nice, as if he were a glowing, fragrant gas. "I read somewhere he has a ranch in Montana," she offers.

"Did he come on to you?"

Pallas shrugs. "I think he was, you know, into me."

"Did you make a date with him?"

"His bodyguard told me to, like, call him." She doesn't seem surprised by this invitation, but neither is she displeased.

"You called his *bodyguard*?"

"No, his bodyguard told me to call Chip."

"So you *do* have his phone number?" Torn between jealousy and professional zeal.

"It's at home somewhere. Anyway, who knows if it's really his right number?"

"Did you meet him after work?" I demand. "You did, didn't you?" I put my head down on the table, distraught. Pallas strokes my head maternally.

"Connor, what do you want from me?"

WHAT HE WANTS FROM PALLAS

What he wants is not exactly sex, although it is surely coextensive with sex. What he wants almost certainly doesn't even exist: the Platonic essence of Pallas. Like goddesses of screen and runway, her inaccessibility is the key to her allure. She is part of his current spiritual crisis—his perverse need to prove himself worthy of Philomena even as he behaves in unworthy fashion. In reflective moments he tells himself that he wants to prove to Pallas that love exists, that there is another model besides the purely mercenary one she subscribes to, in which case he might be able to believe that Philomena could love him in spite of his own negligible market value.

According to Plato, love is the desire for the good; yet it's hard to see how his desire for Pallas can lead to anything but trouble. In *The Symposium*, Aristophanes defines us, qua lovers, as human sores seeking to be healed. Connor has not yet quite determined how to remain true to Philomena even as he yearns for something else. Neither Brooke, with all her powers of reasoning, nor even the great Sophists Protagorus and Gorgias, might be able to crack this one.

WHAT YOU SETTLE FOR

"Would you like me to dance," she asks, still stroking your hair. You answer by thumping your head against the table. It's the best you can do, for now. She rises and slowly shimmies her dress down over her shoulders, down the articulate ridge of her clavicles and up the rising slope of her chest until are revealed those breasts which, even here in this Mammary Hall of Fame, are to your mind among the chief wonders of the modern world, not least because they were shaped by nature and gravity. No little scars underneath. In addition to her current employment at Mount Olympus, Pallas is also a breast model for several prominent cosmetic surgeons. Once she begins to dance you see illustrated in the most striking fashion various laws of physics which, of all your wide acquaintance, only Brooke could identify by name.

THE MOLE PEOPLE

There are people who live underground, in the pipes and tunnels beneath the city. Thousands of them—their children growing up in the dark, their childish eyes becoming weaker, their noses and nostril hairs longer, afraid of the bright surface light. Life became too complicated on the surface. Broken water mains create subterranean oases. Perhaps this is what Philomena means by the simple life.

WHY THE JAPANESE MAKE SUCH GOOD CARS AND SELDOM KILL EACH OTHER

One of the things that you admire about the Japanese, collectively, is that it hardly occurs to them to ask *why*. But, whatever you might once have thought, back in Kyoto in your snug little *uchi*, wearing your woolen *hakata*, wooden geta on your feet, you are not, nor will you ever be, Japanese. You arrived with the teleological itch already in place.

Your sister could learn plenty from the Japanese.

THE WRITER AT HOME

Finding myself on the Upper West Side the following afternoon— having interviewed an actress on Central Park West (boring, please, don't ask)—I decide to drop in on Jeremy. (Well, all right, you slavering sluts, I'll treat you to one quote that's going straight into my programming bank: "I don't consider myself a star. I'm just proud to be part of an artistic community" (SHIFT, *Bloomsbury*).

Jeremy buzzes me in, watches me through the slot of the stair-well as I trudge up five flights.

"Dude ascending a staircase," he says, his long blond hair hanging halfway to the fourth floor. He nods grimly, precedes me inside, then collapses on the chaise in his impeccably neat, plant-infested living room. I sense wintry gloom amidst the verdure.

"You must be the man from the suicide hotline."

"Nope. President of the Jeremy Green Fan Club."

"You lie. It disbanded shortly after *Slender Mercies* was remaindered. Two of its members went into group therapy and the other one ditched me for the Dennis Johnson Fan Club." Jeremy sighs and squirms; though you might think a handsome writer sprawled on a chaise would evoke the young Truman Capote, Jeremy calls to mind a man being stretched and tortured on the rack by invisible inquisitors.

"Look at this," he demands, shoving a copy of the *Daily News* under my nose. There, in the "On the Town" section, is a photo of a glowering Jeremy and a beaming Philomena at the benefit.

"Congratulations," I say.

"I'm fucking mortified."

"Is that a comment on my girlfriend?"

"She's a model. Fine for her to stand around grinning at the camera—that's her job. I'm a *writer*, for Christ's sake."

"One picture in the paper doesn't necessarily compromise your artistic integrity."

"They'll never review me seriously again."

Jeremy is so fastidious and fearful of seeming to promote himself at the expense of the words on the page that he has refused his editor's offer of a publication party. He professes a horror of the wet kiss of popular taste, although he bitterly resents his obscurity vis-à-vis certain writers he considers far less talented. Favorably reviewed in the Sunday *Times Book Review*, and *The New Yorker* (in brief), his debut collection sold some forty-five hundred copies in hardcover, respectable numbers for a story collection in which suicide is a major theme; and while he likes to say there are only five thousand serious readers of fiction in the entire Republic, I have also heard him speak libelously about the sales force of his former publishing house. His forthcoming collection is called *Walled-In*, a gloss on Thoreau—with a nod to Poe's "Cask of Amontillado"—in which the island of Manhattan serves as a dystopian mirror for the pond of Walden, a septic ecosystem which drives its inhabitants to despair and suicide. I keep asking for a galley, but he insists that I wait for the finished book.

Standing up, he paces the room and sighs eloquently. "Is there something they tell everybody else about how to wake up in the morning and actually *want* to get out of bed? Something I missed at the portal of this last incarnation? Is there some reward that I don't know about for not just killing yourself?"

"I think it's called sex."

"Easy for you to say. You live with the cover girl, you bastard. Me, I can't even get my fucking dog back." Jeremy sticks his finger in one of the numerous flowerpots, frowns, walks to the kitchen. Actually, Philomena has never been on the cover of anything—has in fact semiretired from the modeling profession to become an actress—and Jeremy has women heaving themselves across his path, clutching his ankles, weeping at the sight of him, begging for his phone number, a lock of hair, a drive-by sperm deposit. Imagine a rock star with great skin and teeth and an astounding vocabulary to boot. Most men walking around inside of Jeremy's epidermis would find multiple reasons to be happy. As for Jeremy's former canine companion, it's a long, sad story. He emerges with a watering can, which he applies to the ficus.

"I thought you were getting the beast back last week."

Uh-oh, sorry I asked. Jeremy appears ready to burst into tears. Turning from me, paying particular attention to the thirsty ficus.

A   B O Y   A N D   H I S   D O G

Sean was a spirited Irish terrier who liked to chew shoes and bark at the roaches which have the free run of Jeremy's apartment. Sean was purchased after the demise of Mulligan, Jeremy's beloved companion of thirteen years. After nearly a year with Sean, Jeremy decided he hadn't recovered from the death of Mulligan, and that it was not fair to treat Sean as a surrogate. Moreover, he concluded that it was a crime to keep a dog, particularly one as feisty and energetic as Sean—who could perform a triple axel on hardwood— walled in, as it were, in a one-bedroom apartment in New York City. So he took out ads in *Newsday* and the *Bergen County Record* soliciting a good country home for Sean, envisioning a New Jersey farm with rolling fields to run and rabbits to harass. Waiting for the responses to pour in, he debated the relative chemical toxicity of New Jersey versus Long Island. Finally, after interviewing all three callers, and visiting homes in Patchogue and Nyack, Jeremy selected the Jamisons, a childless couple living near Flemington,

New Jersey. The Jamisons—Bob and Edie—agreed that Jeremy could visit once a month.

Returning home on the New Jersey Turnpike, Jeremy realized the enormity of his mistake. Distraught, he pulled over on the shoulder of the Pike to catch his breath and scarf a Klonopin. But he sucked it up and tried to convince himself that Sean was better off, waiting three whole days before calling, whereupon he asked the Jamisons to put the phone to Sean's ear. The following Sunday he drove out to Flemington and stayed for two hours, in spite of the three-week hiatus specified by the original agreement. When he returned again the following Sunday, it is to be imagined that the Jamisons thought they were seeing rather more of Jeremy than they'd prefer. All I have is Jeremy's testimony: that he couldn't sleep, couldn't write, missed Sean and wanted him back. Moreover, on one of his visits he had discovered, having perused the reading matter displayed on the coffee table, that Mr. Jamison was an ardent firearms enthusiast and hunter. He told the Jamisons he'd changed his mind, which fact did not seem relevant to them, a deal being a deal. Sensing he had their number, Jeremy offered money. They agreed to five hundred dollars and then demurred. He raised his offer to a thousand. They promised they'd get back to him.

This began almost six months ago. Ongoing negotiations reveal—if Jeremy is to be believed, and let me say right now that my best friend gives new depth and resonance to the concept of an unreliable narrator—that Mrs. Jamison is quite a brilliant sadist. The husband professes himself willing to surrender the dog, but leaves the details to the little woman, who seems to delight in tortured, elaborate negotiations that somehow break down at the last minute. Only the combined ministrations of Jeremy's shrink and his guru have kept him intact, and perhaps preserved Mrs. Jamison's life. But in truth she is sorely testing Jeremy's credo of nonviolence.

The watering can empty, Jeremy walks over to his answering machine, rewinds the tape, presses REPLAY:

MESSAGE FROM THE DOG MOTHER

"Hello, this is Edie Jamison. I know you sit there and listen to people talking into your machine. You're probably there right now, with your ridiculous self-important hair, listening to me. Does it make you feel superior to have people talk while you pretend not to be there, like that writer in your story? That's just the kind of thing someone like you would do, isn't it? You think people don't see through you but they do. Oh yes, they certainly do. I read your so-called book, you know. What do your poor parents feel about what you write? How do they feel about that sewage? I bet they're ashamed to walk down the street. If I were your mother, I'd be disgusted with myself for raising a spoiled know-it-all ungrateful brat who can't even take care of his dog, who gives his poor dog away and who thinks he can just walk into people's lives and offer them some money to make everything the way he wants. Well, let me tell you something, my husband may be a pushover, but I'm not. You think you're so superior—"

Enraged afresh, Jeremy jerks the plug out of the answering machine.

"What," I ask, "was your latest offer?"

"Two grand."

"Hell, *I'll* be your dog for that."

Jeremy's face clearly expresses the information that he does not find this even a little bit amusing.

THE BUDDHA OF WEST SIXTY-NINTH

Jeremy does have an unreliable sense of humor. Perhaps partly because he is as acutely sensitive to his own suffering as my sister is to that of others. Whatever residual sympathy Jeremy can spare is donated not to humans but to other life-forms—from mammals to insects—a fact which I try to keep in mind when I am tempted to reach out and squash the roaches that roam the apartment as freely and abundantly as buffalo in the Old West. Jeremy not only refuses to kill them himself, but he also bars the landlord's exterminator, with the result that all the roaches in the building, knowing a good deal when they smell one, have migrated up here to the top floor.

"What does your swami say?"

"Swami say—'It sometimes veddy veddy tricky to tell dog from man. Also, veddy veddy hard to justify ways of dog to man.'" Jeremy's fluent ability to ridicule his swami even as he reveres him, even as he arranges his life in accordance with the master's gnomic instructions, has always puzzled me. The swami actually convinced him once to take a vow of celibacy for six months. Maybe Philomena has been consulting the old fraud.

I am unable to persuade him to come out for lunch. Not even the invocation of lentils and kasha and other vile fibrous fare at the nearby hippie vegetarian boîte can turn the trick. When I pull the door behind me, Jeremy is once again sprawled over the chaise, as if on a bed of nails.

THE IMPORTANCE OF JOHN GALLIANO

Back home, strangely, no message from Philomena, but one from Connor's boss, Jillian Crowe, asking for an update on the Chip Ralston situation. Chip was Jillian's idea of an idea. She had seen him, the young thespian, a few weeks ago at the Bryant Park fashion shows, checking out the models. The notion of a profile came as an afterthought during an editorial meeting at which Jillian declared that John Galliano might well be the most important artist of the latter half of the century. And this at a meeting of the Features Department, as opposed to Fashion. Beautifully tonsured heads, Jillian's courtiers, bobbing assent all around the conference room table. In the realm of fashion, where breathless enthusiasm sings harmony with toxic ennui, Jillian has perfect pitch; she's like a publicist on smack, and cannot for the life of her understand why she has not yet been tapped to edit *Vogue* or *Harper's Bazaar*.

CONNOR AMONG THE PLUTOCRATS

There was a moment when Connor seemed to have the knack of pleasing Princess Jillian, a twinkling when he detected an almost girlish interest in both his person and his so-called work, culminating when he escorted her—a last-minute substitute for Boaz Mazor, but an escort nonetheless—to the Costume Institute Ball at the Metropolitan Museum. This was the metropolis as it was meant to be seen, in the flattering aphrodisiac light of eminence, a brilliant oligarchy compounded of wealth, power, accomplishment and beauty. The atmosphere of festive mutual regard extended even to tourists, such as Connor, on the happy assumption that their applications for full-fledged citizenship were pending. He was with Jillian Crowe, therefore he was. If he'd first taken the whole thing more or less as a joke, secure in his self-knowledge as a flunky and a last-minute, anomalous, heterosexual walker—toward the end of the night he was nevertheless beginning to feel remarkably comfortable in this new role.

Infected with a desire to please and fortified with half a dozen glasses of champagne, he regaled the table with colorful anecdotes about Japanese sexual practices and the untold story behind a recent celebrity interview. He expounded his theory that there are exactly two kinds of movie star, the Solipsist and the Seducer: one speaks only of himself, not believing in the existence of anyone else; the other still seems not to believe in his or her own existence at all and has to seek constant verification from every possible fan in the room, working it like a politician, looking into the great round mirrors of our eyes, trying to seduce us all one at a time. Al Pacino was sitting at the adjacent table, and Jillian was apparently offended on his behalf, which was silly, in Connor's view, since he wasn't remotely listening to anything anyone else said anyway, at his own table or elsewhere.

Connor doesn't think Jillian appreciated this performance quite as much as he'd hoped she might. Truthfully, he doesn't exactly remember. Perhaps—it's possible—he drank too much. He does recall her saying "Darling, when I offer to show you the *ropes*, do try to pick up more than *just* enough to hang yourself."

And then came Philomena's reaction: irate at the datelike aspects of what Connor tried to present as a tedious professional obligation. Strictly a court eunuch, Connor assured her. "Why don't you ask Jillian to fuck you" became a late-night refrain in their bedroom for quite some time. "I'm sure she'd be happy to oblige—if she hasn't already."

It seemed to Connor that he paid dearly for this little outing on both fronts, at home and at work. Re the latter: perhaps his novelty simply wore off, novelty being the cardinal virtue in the value system of the magazine; or perhaps Jillian realized he despised his job. At any rate, after that night, the frisson fizzled between Connor and Jillian Crowe. Short of assassinating Anna Wintour, he can't quite imagine how to regain Jillian's esteem.

AN OMEN?

Also, besides the Crowe call, a message from Mrs. Combes, ancient West Village bohemian landlady who used to hang out with Edna St. Vincent Millay: "Hello? Hello? Is this working? Oh, dear, I hate these things. Well, if anyone can hear me, this is Sharon Combes. Mr. McKnight, I've been calling your, uh, Miss Briggs on the number I have for her but she hasn't, uh, called me back. I'm sure there's some mistake, but her rent is almost a month overdue. It's the twenty-third today. And she's always been so prompt, I usually get her check the last day of the month, sometimes on the first or second, which I really appreciate since it takes five days for the check to clear and I've got the heating bill and the mortgage and . . ."

Pouring yourself a large tumbler of Jack Daniel's in order to drown the rambunctious colony of moths in your belly.

Y E L L O W

Jeremy calls, furious with John Cheever. In his journal, a portion of which has just been published in the *Paris Review*, Cheever had some unkind things to say about bitterness, and Jeremy is taking it personally, although the offending remarks are actually directed at J. D. Salinger.

"Listen to this," Jeremy shouts into the phone. " 'His prose is excellent and supple but he seems very close to crazy. I am reminded of the bitterness in my own work, that bitterness that is not art but that is its opposite. So I would like to write a story that is all yellow, yellow, yellow, the brightest yellow.' " Jeremy is indignant. "Where's all this goddamned bitterness in Cheever? A little bitterness would have been welcome."

Cheever has slandered one of Jeremy's favorite emotions. He tends to read all literary criticism as thinly veiled commentary on his own work. Salinger is one of his secret totems, and when Cheever assails him, however mildly, he might just as well kick Jeremy Green directly in the balls.

"*Yellow, yellow, yellow,*" Jeremy sneers. "What is he—a fucking Nip? Give me a break. Céline should have felt *less bitter?* Would that have made him a greater artist? What about Evelyn Waugh?"

"Foreigners," I point out. "Euros always do cynicism better."

M I L A N ,   I T A L Y ,   F A L L   ' 9 5

Re: Yellow. There exists a mustardy, light-starved, paradoxical, melancholy shade of this most cheerful hue found only in Milan. Connor once went there with Philomena, during the spring collections, to write a profile of an actress who just had to get a sneak preview of the new Versaces. Business. And pleasure. Oh, yes. One night after drinks in the Four Seasons, Philomena had challenged him to take her right there, in the Via Gesù, against the yellow stucco palazzo. *Come on, do me.* Leaning against the wall, her tongue in his ear. The street momentarily deserted. Bittersweet

Campari on her lips. "Come on," she said, licking his ear. "Pretend I'm a hooker. A streetwalker." Earlier, in the bathroom of the Four Seasons, she'd encountered two Russian prostitutes, just off the plane, changing into their best and painting their faces, comparing notes on the men in the bar. Returning to their table with the tale, she could see that it excited him.

Now, on the street, this was her challenge: "Right here, right now."

"Here?" But he was already lifting her skirt, lowering his fly, enfolding her in the tent of his camel's hair coat, cradling her cool ass and scraping his knuckles raw against the stucco. A couple passed, hugging the far side of the narrow street, but by then Connor didn't care. He wasn't there. He was somewhere far more beautiful than Milan by then.

Venice, at the very least.

GOTHAM, FALL '96

When I ask Jeremy to dinner, he claims he's too bummed out. (You might even color him bitter.) In desperation I offer to submit to culinary high-fiber horror on the Upper West Side, but he is still engaged in the World Wrestling Federation's Short Story title bout. Cheever in tights, yanking Jeremy's long blond mane. Jeremy tagging Salinger, who leaps into the ring and stubs out his cigarette on Cheever's backside. Updike in a rabbit suit outside the ropes, waiting to spell Cheever.

Did I mention that Jeremy's still trying to get over the revelation of Cheever's bisexuality? For him it was not a moral question, but a personal one: he wondered if he might be missing out on some crucial component of literary experience by virtue of not sleeping with men. We spent many nights parsing this subject; also, the subject of whether he should try heroin. Because I'd snorted it a couple of times he considered me an authority. I didn't try to dissuade him with the notion that it was dangerous, which after all was the whole point, the authenticating virtue. The real problem, I told him, was that it was so damn fashionable—the cool recreational choice of young Hollywood's hottest—knowing this would chill his Shaker heart.

"As a fiction writer," I say, "it behooves you to get out in the world more, fill up the old well. Coming out to dinner with me is a good start."

"I'm too depressed to face a room full of masticating yuppies. And I can't handle a night of staring across the table at your girlfriend. It's too fucking depressing looking at her across the table, thinking *you're* going home with her."

"*Pas de* sweat. She's in San Francisco on an audition."

"Are you crazy? Don't you have any idea what goes on around movie sets?"

"She's not on a set. She's just auditioning. Or maybe a shoot." Suddenly I realize that the actual nature of the trip was never quite specified.

"So I guess you've never heard of the casting couch."

"I trust her, okay?"

"Don't say I didn't warn you. Sex is the medium and the currency of that racket. That's what she's selling. I mean, being a model is, like, acceptable on a certain level if you're a beautiful girl like Philomena and you just sort of slide into it while you're figuring out what to do with your life. But a model who aspires to be an actress—that's a premeditated cliché. That's culpable."

"It's not exactly up to me, Jeremy. She's a grown-up."

"Anyway, I think she's moving against the flow of the culture. Models are the apex of consumer society. Pure image. Actors have to speak. They have to simulate personality. They have to actually *do* something. Pater said that poetry aspires to the condition of music. I think modern celebrity aspires to the condition of pure image. Modeling is the purest kind of performance, uncomplicated by content."

"I think Phil," I say, "is *looking* for a little content in her life. As aren't we all?"

"Just don't come crying to me after she's started fucking the director."

And so my best friend succeeds in darkening my night. I dial in some Vietnamese spring rolls, so as not to be away from the phone when Philomena calls from San Francisco. Which, now that I think about it, is far too picturesque and foggy and sung about for its own good—or for mine. A red light flashes through the slats of the shades from the nursing home. A sign? Of what, precisely? Eventually I check the ringer on the phone, call my own number from Philomena's to make sure it's working, then check the dial tone—a high and lonesome sound that echoes through all of the empty spaces inside of me.

ONANISTIC INTERLUDE

Connor masturbates, replaying the previous day's erotic encounter—a fresh entry in the memory bank—as an act of magic, perhaps, to bring her closer, to conjure her back. This is his own special form of fidelity—the fact that Philomena is his exclusive muse in this department. It must be love, he reasons, if after three years you still, and only, beat off to the image of your girlfriend. Though embarrassment has prevented him from sharing this information with the object of his desire. When she returns, he decides, he will tell her. He will open his heart, amend his life, strive to be the man for her that he has so far failed to be.

Amen.

EXTERIOR

No phone messages when I awake. Outside, a trio of old folks bundled against the cold in their wheelchairs, optimistically facing the silver November sun. Gingerly venturing outside for cappuccino and a chocolate croissant to help me face the day, I sidestep a giant pink-and-white bone with pendant flesh outside the bakery—the thigh of a mastodon by the look of it.

On the corner, waiting for the light, babe in a wheelchair; very chic, black coat and skirt, tiger-striped black-and-gold hair under a

beret, Doc Martens perched on the silver footrests. The first love of
the morning. Fall in love at least twelve times a day. But you, my
dear, are absolutely my first love on wheels. . . .
     Across the street two cops loitering.
     "Matthew Broderick."
     "I didn't see that one."
     "No, that was him. Just now."
     "No shit?"

E - M A I L

Congratulations, Mr. McKnight. "*You've got mail!*" My computer
talks to me.

To: Scribbler
From: Lawgirl
Subject: Lazy White Folks
Dear Connor:
What's with Brooke? She wigging out on us again? Can't get the
girl to return my calls or e Mail. Will you *please* tell her to check
in ASAP? Or am I gonna have to come down and beat the shit
out of you both? Tell her I don't think I can make Christmas this
year, cause Uncle Errol's real sick in Freeport and I got to go see
the old bastard whiles I still can. Gotta go. Loved your insightful,
sensitive piece on Judd Nelson.
Your loving sister,
Corvetta

Nice to see that the fine art of personal correspondence isn't dead
yet. Have I mentioned Corvetta? Her Bahamian parents worked
the orange groves as migrant pickers, until her father sliced her
mother's stomach open with a cane knife. It happened right in
front of Brooke and Corvetta, who were playing outside the trailer
at the time. I don't remember any of this, but my parents tend to
date Brooke's almost pathological sense of empathy from this

event. Corvetta, on the other hand, having so violently lost her mother, grew up tough as . . . well let's just say she grew up to be a lawyer. As though, in that moment when the blade flashed and disappeared into Corvetta's mother, Brooke conveyed all of her own psychic armor to her friend.

Brooke could never understand why my parents didn't adopt Corvetta. A few days after the murder, in an attempt to persuade them, she conducted her first hunger strike. Corvetta was eventually raised by relatives, but she spent summers and Christmas holidays with us, and my parents paid for her education. With Brooke's fierce encouragement she eventually graduated from Harvard, where they roomed together, and went on to distinguish herself at the law school. Brooke's best friend from age three to this very day, she now practices criminal law in Oakland, having turned out better than her friends in the big house, Brooke and me, casualties of privilege.

MORE E-MAIL

To: Scribbler@aol.com
From: Jenrod@inch.com
Subject: A Fan!
Dear Connor:
Is it okay if I call U Connor, Mr. Scribbler? I got your address from the "Contributor's Notes" at the front of the magazine. Have you noticed how most of the good E mail names are already taken? My actual name is Jennifer Rodriguez but I'm thinking about changing it. That's one of the things I want to ask you about. But first before you start thinking who is this crazy grrrl and why is she e mailing me let me just say I am a HUGE FAN! (That doesn't mean I'm FAT on the contrary I'm quite slim!) I don't know if writers have "fans" or not but in your case they should! I mean, writing could be considered a talent just like acting or singing. Maybe I could start a Connor McKnight "fan club." Except I'd rather keep you to myself for now. (Just kidding!)

I especially loved your interview last month on Jennifer Lopez, not just because we share the same first name and are both Latinas (Half, anyway, my Mom is Irish). I really felt like you got inside her head. Anyway it must be really cool getting to meet so many interesting stars and celebs and spending "quality time" with them. Some articles you don't really know what that person is really like, it just sounds like HYPE with a capital H! but your articles really make me feel like I get to know the people. But I bet you're just as interesting yourself. It's not just the Stars who have fascinating personalities although we might not all be famous! Your "head shot" in front of the magazine last month was really cute, I bet you could be a movie star yourself! Believe it or not people say that to me! And not just my mother. (Ha Ha!) Maybe I will send U my picture anyway. I caught the "acting bug" playing Molly in "The Unsinkable Molly Brown" in junior high and since then I have taken classes and my teachers say I have real potential. One of the things that interests me about reading about the stars is how they got their big breaks. I'm still waiting for my big break it seems like its all about "who you know" and "connexions" instead of natural born talent. Plus which being half Dominican which I use to think was against me but now with Jennifer Lopez and Daisy Fuentes and whoever I feel like may be I have a chance. I have also noticed that modelling is a "stepping stone" to an acting career certainly in the case of Rene Russo that is true although after seeing Cindy Crawford in that movie with Billy Baldwin I am not so sure! (Two thumbs down from Jennie Rodriguez.) May be we could meet some time for coffee. I can come to Manhattan anytime except for Tues and Thurs nights which are my acting class. Have you heard of Don Garrison? He's my teacher he had a part on "Saved by the Bell" as well as several major theatrical productions. Oh well guess I have been rambling on enough about me. What about you? E me! PS Don't worry, nobody reads my E mail except me, myself and I.

FALL

Yellow leaves fluttering down the face of the building across the street, like messages from a princess in a high tower. The putrid, wino-vomit smell of gingko leaves underfoot in the Village. Another year sliding past.

DEMI-TASSE

Demi Moore on the cover of *Beau Monde* again. But, hey, it's a whole new twist—she's wearing clothes. Although her head is naked this time, shorn stubbly for a movie she's shooting. For those of you who have just immigrated from Kigali, Demi Moore is a person who is paid twelve million dollars a pop to impersonate fictional characters on-screen. *Beau Monde* is a late-twentieth-century glossy magazine devoted to naked pictures of Demi Moore as well as articles about:

1. International affairs
2. Demi: the woman behind the mask
3. La Dolce Vita
4. What it's like when two international superstars (Demi and Bruce Willis, her famously temperamental former-bartender hubby) share the same house!
5. The Literary Life
6. How Demi knew from the time she was a little girl that she would someday be a star
7. Sex Lives of the Saints
8. Demi's body: how she *feels* about it
9. The British Royal Family and the lesser peerage
10. How *everybody* knew from the time she was a little girl that she would someday be a star, despite her *childhood demons*
11. Lives of the Supermodels

12. How Motherhood is more important to Demi than anything (CTRL, *baby*). Well, almost anything
13. The Media
14. Demi's opinion of narrative modalities in *The Charterhouse of Parma*
15. The beau monde
16. Demi's opinions on the prospects for long-term peace in the Balkans
17. Madonna
18. Demi's body: how we *feel* about it
19. Glowing profiles of fashion designers who happen to be major advertisers
20. Meta Demi: learned asides about the way in which previously published photographs of and articles about Demi in *Beau Monde* have modified and amplified her legend

RELEVANT DISCLOSURE

Your commentator has twice been turned down for a job at *Beau Monde*. But this does not, in his own opinion, unduly prejudice his comments on this particular subject: he's been turned down by practically every publication in town from *Sassy* to *Foreign Affairs*.

PERSONAL DEMONS

Hard to shake the feeling that Demi Moore is following me around. I saw her at Mount Olympus just a few weeks ago. Once there were guardian angels and patron saints; now we have Celebrity Nemeses. Come on now, it's not just me. You have one, surely. Some celeb whose accomplishments, fame, riches and choice of sleeping partners affront you in a deeply personal way, who makes you hurl your copy of *People* magazine across the room in anger. "Basically, I just think of myself as an ordinary person whose job happens to be acting/singing/getting my picture taken" (ALT, *unglam*).

And where the hell is Chip Ralston, boy movie star, god-damnit? His demon publicist, Judith Viertel, will not return my calls. I have actually succeeded in finding the unlisted number at Chip's beach house in Malibu, but all I get is a machine with a viscous, groin-tingling female voice. "No one is here to take your call right now, please leave a message and someone will get back to you real soon. Have an excellent day." For some reason I imagine this to be the voice of my new e-mail correspondent.

SUSPICIOUS INFORMATION

Connor calls his girlfriend's modeling agency to ask for the name of her hotel in San Francisco.

"San Francisco?" says the booker. "What's in San Francisco? I show no booking for Philomena in San Francisco. In fact, I'm showing no bookings at all. She booked out. Told me she was taking the week off."

Connor feels a painful outward pressure on either side of his skull, above and behind the ears, as if he were growing horns.

NEUTRAL INFORMATION, i.e., RAW DATA

Philomena Briggs, born Oklahoma City, Oklahoma, 13 July 1971. Height: 5'10". Hair: auburn. Dress size: 4. Shoe size: 8. Measurements: 34-24-34.

INTERPRETATION

The above data come from her composite, the photo-illustrated business card distributed by Phil's modeling agency, and in fact is not raw at all but cooked to a turn. The actual birth date is 1969. The place of birth was a town too small to show up on any map. The measurements are obviously suspect. And the last time I bought her a dress I had to return the 4 to Barney's and get the 6.

"The salesclerk told me they ran small," I noted helpfully as she tried it on, knowing that if she got upset with the way she looked in it, I might not get lucky for days. Not to mention the danger to nearby ceramics and glassware.

HOW I GOT MY JOB

The joke around the office is that Jillian Crowe, our beloved editrix in chief, gave me the celeb beat at *CiaoBella!* after she heard that I was living with a model named Phil. Another point in my favor was the suit I wore for my interview, a vintage Brooks Brothers gray-flannel hand-me-down from the Dad; Jillian thought I was fashion forward enough to have anticipated the return of the three-button sack suit. She has since discovered her mistakes, and observed my relative lack of starfucking passion. Also, I lost popularity throughout the office when I refused to get behind the seventies revival, my contention being that it's bad enough that many of us will have to look at snapshots of ourselves in those clothes, in those shoes, with those haircuts, every time we pull out the old family album for the rest of our lives. For entirely different reasons I am dreading the inevitable upcoming eighties revival. Big-shouldered knights in matte Armani.

At the mag, it is a source of collective shame that I possess not a single item of apparel bearing the Prada or Gucci logos. Flyers for sample sales are left on my desk with the notation *FYI*.

My contract is up at the end of the year, less than six weeks away. No one has approached me about renewal. My cubicle on the "editorial" floor has been gradually, inexorably, encroached by storage space; I am in the vanguard of the virtual-office concept, faxing in my copy via modem from my apartment. Each time I return bodily to the magazine I find that the partition defining my space has been moved yet again; there is now room for only my desk and chair. Perhaps I should read this month's feature, "The Nine Secrets of Office Life." For example, number 2: "Don't be a loner; the workplace is no place for rugged individualism, girlfriend!"

Our office is a tidal pool of feminine hormones. Svelte Harrison James, the only full-time male on premises, often volunteers his services as a fitting model for in-office shoots. As a straight male I am viewed as the urban equivalent of the village idiot—harmless, perhaps, but kind of a communal embarrassment. My only institutional credibility derives from my association with Phil, whose picture has several times graced both ad and editorial pages.

ENTER, PHIL

I met her in Tokyo, on the Ginza Line between Akasaka-Mitsuke and Shimbashi. For more than six years I had been seeking something in Japan. Maybe, after all, it was a girl from the American Southwest.

One pivotal morning in Kyoto I woke up feeling like a stranger on the planet, so peculiar and senseless did the previous course of my life seem to me. Having lost the faith necessary to maintain my arcane pursuit of Japanese literature, I embraced the ostensible simplicity of Zen. And then, after seven months of zazen in a Kamakura monastery, I decided that neither was I ready to leave behind the world of multiplicity and illusion. Spotting Philomena within two months of hanging up my robe struck me as a vindication of that sentiment. If not satori, it was nevertheless a lightning bolt of a sort.

I couldn't help noticing her, of course, the only other gaijin in the subway car, a head taller than the indigenous population, her black modeling portfolio clutched defensively to her chest. My impression, in that context, was that she was the embodiment of a kind of American beauty which I had almost forgotten the look of, and for the first time in many months I felt homesick, trying very hard not to stare. As pretty as she was, I also believed I could see more than anyone else could—a secret aspect to her beauty that spoke specifically to me. And I felt aggrieved imagining that she would soon pass out of my sight forever. "From the point of view of knowledge," says Kashiwagi the clubfoot in Mishima's *Temple of the Golden Pavilion*, "beauty is never a consolation." At that moment I felt like the cripple, staring at the golden temple. I looked away, embarrassed, after she suddenly met my riveted gaze.

"Excuse me? Do you know which stop is Ginza?"

I took my time, following an entire, meaningless line of print across the page of my *Cinema Nippon* before looking up. I wanted to say, "What makes you assume I speak English." After all these years in Japan I stupidly liked to imagine I blended in somehow. And I was still angry at her for the way she looked. But I was struck earnest by her expression, which seemed suspended between the poles of all-American ingenuousness and the wariness of the pretty woman.

ATTACK OF THE FIVE-FOOT SALARYMAN

Somehow finding my voice, I told her Ginza was the next stop. She turned away, and I felt helpless to pursue my advantage, paralyzed by awe and shyness, forty seconds from losing sight of her forever when an unlikely hero came to my rescue. Stealthily glancing at the juncture of her skirt and her thigh, I saw a hand reach out and pinch her butt. She squealed, and I moved forward protectively. *Anata no kobun shiteru,* I said to the man, who looked at me agog—a talking gaijin. I took her arm, leading her away to a symbolically safe distance.

"What did you say to him," she asked, once we were seated in the coffee shop outside the station.

"I told him I knew his boss," I said. "Which is roughly the equivalent, cross-culturally speaking, of telling an American lech that you know his wife. The censure of wives not counting for much around here."

AN OKIE ABROAD

Refugee from a small town in Oklahoma, Philomena was in Japan trying to build up her modeling portfolio and savings account.

She'd been in the country two months, sharing a flat with three other girls. Hers was a hardscrabble childhood at best. Something of a wimp myself, I admired her gutsiness. She was the kind of girl who could cut in line without pissing anybody off. *Hey, you don't mind do you, thanks a lot. See, I told you he wouldn't mind.* Not many guys would have minded being cut in front of by Phil. She had a look which made you feel you'd been physically touched, and she was not at all unconscious of her power. She'd learned to use what had been given to her.

THE FIRST TIME

Having already illustrated Philomena's drawbacks as a sexual partner, or rather as an intended sexual partner, I should give credit where it's due: the first night she went home with me I judged that everything I previously had called sex was a pale imitation of the Platonic form of fucking I experienced under Philomena's supervision. It started badly, or so I thought; sitting on the floor of my chilly apartment sipping tea, she told me about previous boyfriends, including one that she had "shared" with a friend.

"I used to see this guy at the gym," she said, "and he was so hot. We used to check each other out. But we never talked. One day we were leaving together. And without a word he just followed me home, threw me down on the bed. This happened a few times. And then one day I was eating lunch with my girlfriend Cindy, telling her about this guy—and there he was in the restaurant, looking at me. I got up to go the ladies' and he followed. Just followed me right into the stall and closed the door. What was so great was it was just sex. Nothing else."

I wanted her to stop and yet it was too late, it was like watching a car going slowly over a cliff; I felt powerless to intervene or turn away.

"It was too good not to share," she continued. "I told him to wait. And I went back to the table and told Cindy to go the ladies' room. It was like telling your best friend about a great sample sale."

True or not, this story so unmanned me that Philomena would

have passed out of my life untouched if she hadn't carped the diem that night. But now I realize she knew exactly what she was doing. She had beaten me down only to raise me up again from despair — on her own terms. When we finally crawled under the sheets of the futon, chaste in our underwear, I was a quivering wreck. For a minute, perhaps five, we lay side by side in the dark. When she reached over and touched my cheek just beneath my ear, I went rigid; when she touched my thigh I had to suppress a sob. I was angry about the story, furious that she'd ever fucked another man, and then for rubbing my nose in it. But I couldn't hold out for long, and she knew it. When she touched my earlobe with the tip of her tongue I began to shake.

I finally lunged at her but she seemed to retreat, drawing away as if she had lost interest. Mad with lust, I attacked again and after a feint-yield she seized command again, rolled over on top of me and commenced torturing me with rhythmic and rationed delights, slowing, pausing just as I began to accelerate, slipping away at the precise moment it seemed that the friction of a single breath would have released me from the bondage of the exquisite filaments in which she had wrapped me.

Once it was finally over, I could have wept with relief and gratitude.

She stroked my hair. "Isn't it sad that it always has to come to an end?"

"The end," I said, "was the best part."

In the dim light of dawn I saw her shake her head. "No," she said. "Somewhere between the middle and the end is always the best part, but we never know exactly where it is until it's over."

Much later, I asked her why she had told me that dreadful story.

"It worked, didn't it?"

"Was it true?"

In response, she reached down and placed her hand on my cock.

WHAT SHE SAW IN CONNOR

Perhaps she was impressed with his knowledge, his fluency with the language. In that stranger-in-a-strange-land context, Connor cut a fairly striking figure, being able to fend off subway pinchers, order food right off the menu—without reference to the plastic models in the windows—count, ask directions and shout insults when necessary (this last no easy feat, Japanese being as impoverished in abusive and obscene words as it is overloaded with honorifics). Which is to say, he doubts she ever would have shacked up with him in the States. His previous amorous history had not been so spectacular as to inspire envy in the heart of his fellow man, and his success in Japan had largely been a function of his novelty: future housewives having a fling with a gaijin. But in the context of adult males known to Philomena, Connor was practically a saint, if only by virtue of having a reasonably pleasant disposition. Her father disappeared when she was three, and of her mother's many boyfriends she would only say that some had been less abusive than others; more than that, she says, whenever asked, he doesn't want to know. There is a room he cannot enter, and indeed he has been afraid to force the door. But in the middle of the night, she has awakened him, pleading with Duane, her stepfather, begging him to stop . . . not that he has ever let on. They live with Duane; he's right there in bed with them, though Connor has never let on that he notices.

After fleeing her mother's house at seventeen, she'd left Oklahoma altogether when her amphetamine-shooting boyfriend suggested that he was willing to share her with paying customers. Her next boyfriend, a photographer who helped her assemble her portfolio when she arrived in New York, had failed to tell her he was married.

Even when she began to speak of a future together, even when they jointly moved back to New York to pursue their shiny dreams, she remained skeptical of Connor's intentions. She found it difficult to imagine Connor might be different from others of his kind.

Though prepared to cast her lot with him, she remained prepared for the worst. Her fatalism sharpened the edge of his yearning. To make her happy became his vocation. And yet the more he tried to convince her he was different from the men of her previous acquaintance, the more he worried that he might not be different enough.

Trying to prove himself worthy, he didn't stop to consider that what she doubted was her *own* worth.

MODEL PSYCHOLOGY

A beauty contest title had been her only ticket out of Oklahoma. Hadn't everyone always told her she could be a model? Hadn't Duane taught her that sex is currency? All the insecurities that she presumably hoped to conquer by exploiting her troublesome, God-given pulchritude were promptly exacerbated by a profession which judged her solely on the basis of those looks; because for every client that booked her, dozens of others found her wanting in comparison with some other girl, providing her with a steady diet of rejection. (*But what was your original face*, goes the famous koan of Huineng, *before you were born?*)

And now—acting. Jesus.

In his fortunate role as boyfriend-of, Connor exempts Philomena from his categorical skepticism vis-à-vis other members of her sorority, whom he occasionally is called upon to interview. ("Actually, I eat pretty much whatever I feel like. I'm like this real junk food junkie. Big Macs, potato chips. I just pig out all the time but for some reason I don't gain a pound"—CTRL, *Eat your hearts out, fat girls.* Or "I was a real ugly duckling as a kid"—ALT, *duck.*)

OFFICE HOURS

Finding the apartment oppressive, I repair to the midtown offices of *CiaoBella!* One message for me with the receptionist. "Check your e-mail from 'A Fan.'" Moments after I sit down in my tiny cubicle, it is invaded by Tina Christian, the advice columnist, our own Ms. Lonelyhearts. Tina is a perpetual-motion machine, a dervish of windmilling limbs and whippy blond hair.

"The big news around the office is the white T," she says, perching her skinny butt on the edge of my desk. "It's, like, a significant trend, the white T. Kate and Christy are wearing them, ditto the girls in the office, in case you haven't noticed. We're doing a spread, Armani is, like, giving a party tomorrow night at his new boutique to celebrate it. *The new simplicity*. The T-shirt. In white. This is what we do for a living."

Thinking of Philomena in a white T-shirt, I sigh.

Tina waves a photograph in my face. "Now, *him* I would like to see in a white T. Or preferably no T. Simplicity itself. The author—in the buff." Closer inspection reveals it to be Jeremy's publicity photo. "Reliable sources tell me," she says, "that you are acquainted with this Byronesque figure. Naturally I scoffed and jeered. 'Connor?' I said. But, hey, I'm willing to be convinced. If you, say, had his home phone number, that would prove that you actually know him, subject to me calling to verify and maybe meeting him for a drink just to make sure he's not a stand-in or impostor you use to impress innocent colleagues."

"Are we," I venture, "reviewing him?"

She cocks her head in dubious contemplation, straightening a paper clip she has plucked from my desk. "Apparently too depressing for our young, bubbly, ambitious, fun-seeking twenty-something readers. At least that's what Bonnie told me. Though I *could* see a possible feature in the well—with pix. What the hell is he so depressed about, anyway? I mean, he looks like a fucking Ralph Lauren model with a functioning brain. But that's okay, I don't mind depression, I love a project, I know I could cheer him up. Did I ever tell you I was cheerleader at Horace Greeley High? God, I am *so* hungover it's not even funny. Were you at the Versace thing last night—and if so can you tell me if I was? You don't have any Advil, do you?"

I hand her the bottle, which I just happen to have in my top drawer.

"So," she says after swallowing a handful, "can you introduce me or what? I could read his manuscripts, collect his Prozac from the pharmacy, fetch his slippers at night."

"Slipper fetching is a touchy subject with Jeremy."

"I suppose you're going to tell me I'm not intellectual enough? Hey, I read the classics at Smith. I own the complete works of Sylvia Plath. I understand symbolism and irony. Irony—advice columnist whose love life sucks."

"I thought you were going out with Kevin Shipley."

"Kevin's such a geek. Though he has his uses. He's, like, the only guy I've ever dated who's short enough to go *up* on me. Which is a good thing because *writer's* block is the least of his problems. I don't know, I just haven't gotten around to dumping him yet."

"Put in a good word for Jeremy before you dump the guy." Kevin being the book reviewer for *Beau Monde*.

"If *I* put in a good word for Jeremy, Kevin will definitely trash him. Poor Tom Beller. I flirted with him one night at a party. It actually didn't even occur to me that Kevin was reviewing his book that week. Whoa, brutality above and beyond the call . . . I mean, anybody under the age of, like, *eighty* who's actually finished a book already has a strike against them in Kevin's mind."

Craning to inspect the correspondence on my desk, she flutters her hand dismissively. "Dating, what a fucking nightmare. It's almost enough to make me stay with Kevin. I just lie back and pretend he's Tom Cruise." She sighs. "What *do* men want, anyway? Don't answer that. It's not like I don't put out. Plus I've been known to give a highly reviewed blow job. It's not like *we* don't want to get laid, too."

Having failed to spot anything interesting on my desk, she stands up and tosses her hair back. "So, are you going to help me out or what?"

"Jeremy is, well, let's just say difficult."

"All I want to know is, is he straight? After that I'll take my chances." Suddenly she jumps in my lap. "Pretty please." She puts her lips against my ear. "Since you refuse to sleep with me, I think it's the least you can do."

"I'll make inquiries."

She kisses me on the lips. "I'll name our firstborn Connor."
Windmilling off, she asks, "How's Phil?"

Fortunately she doesn't wait for the answer. Later, I see that she
has left behind a page from her latest column:

ADVICE FROM TINA C

To Frustrated: Sure, you and your guy have had a little spat. It's
all part of having a RELATIONSHIP. Those twisted conversations that are one part spoken word, one part secret code, one
part mind-reading, one part MALE DUMBNESS, and the next
thing you know you're in your own private Bosnia. Here's a
recipe that'll have him begging to surrender: give the Mouse
Blouse to your little sis and check out the animal print Flirt
Shirts in the GOTTA HAVE column this issue. . . .

TOKYO, AUTUMN 1993

She moved into my tiny flat in Roppongi after the first night. We
slept on a single futon, which we laid out on the tatami floor each
night and folded up each morning. When Philomena went off on
go-sees, I practiced calligraphy and took notes for my Kurosawa
book. Long enamored of the Japanese cinema, after leaving the
monastery I had devoted myself to film, which seemed more
Zen-like in its immediacy than literature. Meanwhile: teaching
English; writing movie reviews for the *Japan Times* and *Tokyo Business Journal*; two evenings a week taking the train to Shinjuku to
conjugate English verbs with Japanese businessmen: *I dump / You
dump / He dumps / We dump / You all dump manufactured goods
below cost on the American market in order to gain market share.*

Once while we were making love the tatami began to tremble
beneath us; the cookware and china came chiming to life in the
kitchen as a shelf of books in the main room toppled to the floor,
narrowly missing the futon.

"Damn, you *are* good," Philomena said, after the last tremor
had subsided.

On free nights cruising the outdoor market for mordant pickled vegetables, anthropomorphic gingerroot, fat talc-y sacks of short-grain rice, bug-eyed fish, skinny chickens with feet. Starting the automatic rice cooker when I heard Philomena's key in the door. We made love when she returned home, and sometimes again after we had rolled out the futon for the night. (Up to now, I might add, the greatest privilege of my uneventful life has been fucking Philomena.) Between tumbles we packed our plastic washbuckets under our arms and set off for the *sento*, the public bath down the street, kissing goodbye at the steaming door as she went in the ladies' side and I in the men's, handing our two hundred yen to an ancient crone whose booth straddled the two worlds. (Ah yes, the public bath, the only place they didn't stare at my *face*.)

After six years I was fairly jaded, but Philomena was new to Japan, and her curiosity and delight reinvigorated my own sense of wonder. In particular, the inversions and ostensible paradoxes delighted her. One day she came home thrilled with the discovery that in Japanese an orgasm is a *going* rather than a *coming*. She kept experimenting with the concept in English. "It's like—honey, don't go in my mouth please." And a few days later: "Do you realize they wash their hands *before* they go to the bathroom?" Every day a revelation for her, and for me a refreshment of perspective.

This might have gone on forever, but within the year we moved to New York—which is to monogamy what the channel changer is to linear narrative.

BREAKFAST ANYTIME

Our first year in New York, however, was as promising as the opening credits of a movie. In fact I wrote it up as a screenplay—though in the screen version we met in the city after arriving with separate and inappropriate partners. Philomena, newly signed to an agency, found everything fresh and excellent. She loved the BREAKFAST ANYTIME sign in the window of our local diner, with its implication that here in the great city you could make up your own schedule, that it was always the beginning of the day in New York. Once she started to get magazine work the Greek owner asked for a photograph, which he framed and hung over the counter among the photos of the soap actors, belly dancers, Matthew Broderick and other neighborhood celebs. *Best to all the gang at the Acropolis, Philomena.*

MAN ON THE WAVE

Sometimes I suspect that since I bailed on academia I have been a ronin, a man on the wave, storm-tossed and unaffiliated.

The role of the samurai was to serve his master. If necessary, to die for him. A samurai who lost his master, for whatever reason, was no longer a samurai but a ronin, his very reason for existence suddenly removed. A masterless samurai was a virtual contradiction in terms, a big-time lost soul.

E-MAIL

To: Jenrod@inch.com
From: Scribbler@aol.com
Subject: Reality
Dear Jennie:
Thank you for your letter. Unfortunately you are quite wrong about me being someone you would want to meet. And the photograph you seem to admire was the work of a very artful dodger with a very expensive camera. As are all the pictures in the magazine. Try not to believe anything you see or read in our little rag, or others like it, and you will be a wiser woman. Delusion, the Zen masters tell us, is the fundamental sickness of human beings. If it is not too late, try to get over "the acting bug." Whatever you do, I wish you well.
Sincerely, Connor McKnight

PHYSICAL APPEARANCE

I suppose you've formed a picture of your protagonist by now, though it occurs to me I haven't been much help in this regard. But then, I've always found the minute portraiture of nineteenth-century fiction fairly useless. For me, those precise descriptions of the hero's nose/mouth/eyes/moles/forehead never come together as an actual face. Maybe it's a failure of synthetic imagination on my part, but in my mind they always end up jumbled, like a portrait in the analytic cubist mode. It's always easier to visualize the minor characters, with their bestial analogues, done in the broad strokes of caricature—Mr. Fox, Mr. Rat, Miss Sheep. Then, too, as a reader I like to take a certain amount of responsibility for filling in the details. I'd be most grateful if you would endow me with rugged, slightly tragic features.

I have actually heard it maintained that beauty is only skin deep; Jillian Crowe, on the other hand, says that appearance is destiny, which is probably closer to the truth. "It's not necessarily whether you win or lose, darling," she once said. "It's how you look while you're playing the game." Something only a born winner—and looker—could say.

Certainly you must have decided by now, for instance, that I am not nearly ambitious enough to be short. Generally it's the taller guys who have the confidence to be fuckups. Actually, until a late spurt of growth when I was fifteen I was small for my age. This hormonal surge was accompanied by a bad case of acne; at the exact moment when sex invaded and colonized my imagination, I couldn't imagine anyone wanting anything physical to do with me. I subsequently attained something more than normal height and my face more or less cleared, though in fact it retains a vaguely lunar aspect to this day.

Several women have claimed that I am more attractive than I think, which surely makes me an extremely rare instance of my sex—men overestimating their physical appeal just about as consistently as women underestimate theirs—and much of the limited success I have enjoyed with women in my youth had the aspect of a pep talk. By now I recognize that brand of womanly pleasure that comes from cheering on the underdog, the nurturing sex's delight in nourishing a pale case of confidence. This, I think, is more relevant than the color of my hair or the shape of my nose.

CELEBRITY SEARCHES

From the office, Connor calls Celebrity Searches, a service to which his magazine subscribes. "Can you give me a current location on Ralston, Chip?"

After three minutes: "Still checking." Finally: "We show him in his Malibu house up until Thursday last week, then we pick him up last Saturday at the Mark in New York. Checked out Monday and we're not showing anything since."

"Can you work on that for me?"

"Sure. Meantime, how about Brad Pitt? He's right here in town. With Gwyneth."

"Who I really need to find is my girlfriend."

"Actress?"

"Model."

"Supermodel?"

"Just a model. Model slash actress."

"Model, nonsuper. Slash actress. Name?"

"Philomena Briggs."

After a search he tells me she's not in their database.

"Could you check the name Fabrizio del Dongo?"

"What, the fashion designer?"

"Protagonist, novel by Stendhal. *Charterhouse of Parma.*"

"Come again?"

WINE NOTES

Guy on the street tries to sell me a bottle of 1976 Lafite Rothschild. Sidles up to me on Eighth Street, wearing those knit gloves with the fingertips amputated to show off his cracked, striated nails, then walks alongside me cradling the bottle as if he were the sommelier at "21" presenting my selection. "Wine of the vintage," he says. "Robert Parker gave it ninety-six points. A quote 'Beautiful bouquet of cedarwood, spices and ripe fruit' unquote. Give it to you for thirty." I wave him off. Actually, I've never been a big Lafite fan. Plus I'm hungover today, for a change.

ANOTHER SPECIAL OFFER, THIS TIME FROM THE PHONE COMPANY

Connor wants to believe in magic. He tells himself that if he can refrain from picking up the phone until the fifth ring, just before the machine picks up—if he can hold out that long he will be rewarded with the sound of Philomena's voice on the other end. But after five rings he is greeted by a nasal honk belonging to an employee of the phone company. The caller wonders if she might explain a limited-time offer—a service package combining call waiting, voice mail and caller ID.

"I have to get off the phone," he says. "I'm expecting a call."

"That's the beauty of call waiting," she says.

"I already have call waiting—wait, hold on a minute. What's this caller ID?"

"A very useful service. Whenever you receive a call your caller's number appears in the window of the special multifeature phone which is free to our customers who sign up for this service before the end of the month."

"I'll take it," Connor says.

PUBLICATION DINNER

Dinner at Da Silvano with Jeremy Green, editor Blaine Forrestal, agent Rachel Salmanson: a celebration of the official publication of Jeremy's new collection of stories tomorrow. The first to arrive, I am shortly joined by Rachel, who does not recognize me. "Hi, it's

Connor," I say helpfully. And then, when this fails to elicit a hearty greeting: "Jeremy's friend."

"Oh right," she says, scanning the room. She's wearing a white T-shirt under, if I'm not mistaken, a Dolce and Gabbana suit. She clearly doesn't approve of the table to which we are escorted, beside the front window, until she is informed that it's Anna Wintour's regular spot.

"The food's actually quite good," she informs me, as if I had disparaged it, or as if, more likely, she assumes I've never dined here before. Tiny and angular, with a permanent air of impatience, she displays the thin blade of her smile as Blaine joins us at the table. "Jeremy's always late," she explains, after the pleasantries have been exchanged.

"Really?" Blaine purses her ample lips. "I've always found him to be extremely prompt. But then I tend to run a little late myself. Hope *you* haven't been waiting long."

SECRETS OF THE LITERARY LIFE

Jeremy arrives direct from the course he teaches at the New School, complaining about his students.

"*You* should teach it," he tells Rachel. "Last week, I'm giving a talk at this community college in Long Island. Of the eight people in attendance: one fell asleep and snored, one left in the middle, and one asked if I could introduce her to my agent, so I did what I always do—since he rejected my first collection—gave her Mort Janklow's home number. And another asks, inevitably, where I get my ideas. I told him there was a 900 number we published writers call for ideas. That's why you need an agent, of course. The only way you can get the number in the first place is from an agent. It's true—you poor buggers—it's all connections! That's what they all secretly believe, anyway. So I tell them: fifty dollars, a hundred dollars and two fifty for a short story idea; two fifty, five hundred and a thousand for novel ideas. Coover's 'The Babysitter,' for example, that's your top-dollar story idea. Ditto Sontag's *The Way We Live*

Now. This business of absorbing the tradition and struggling with the recalcitrance of language doesn't interest them. All they really want is an introduction to my agent."

"Just so long," says Blaine, "as you don't introduce them to your *editor.*"

Even before Jeremy arrived the air was spritzed with the musky whiff of feminine competition between these two women, each of whom feels proprietary about the tortured, handsome young artist. (Reminding me, for some reason, of my very first literary party in New York, a *Paris Review* affair which I attended on Jeremy's coat-tails, when I watched two young men squabbling for the honor of carrying a comatose poet laureate down the stairs.)

L I N E A G E

The slightly tardy star of the evening looks particularly Viking tonight, rampant blond hair hanging halfway down his back. One can see how he doubts his parentage. He refers to his family—his alleged family—as "those people in Oyster Bay." He suspects that a practical joke was played at the portal of his latest incarnation, that he was given the wrong parachute as it were, landing in the midst of a suburban Jewish family, heir to a discount mattress dynasty. Although he possesses a fabulously sensitive instrument for the detection of anti-Semitism—can sense an unspoken slur across vast distances, through closed doors and windows—he nevertheless imagines he should be Irish or possibly Cossack, in the latter case improbably identifying, like the great Isaac Babel, with the folks who tortured and slaughtered his ancestors. When he was twelve Jeremy began attending Catholic Mass, and at fourteen he took his first Communion. In fact the protagonists of his stories tend to bear Irish names. Certainly he doesn't resemble his siblings, two amiable dark-haired fellows who sell mattresses. He keeps trying to get his parents to admit that they adopted him. This makes holidays at the Green household tense. I went there once for dinner and found myself apologizing and virtually translating for the putative eldest son.

A FASHIONABLE CROWD

Our collective attention is captured by movie stars Liam Neeson and Natasha Richardson, who arrive in the company of Sam Cohen, über agent. The volume of conversation drops almost to a whisper, then suddenly rises higher than before, as if it were remote controlled from a dial behind the bar.

"I love the way I'm just sitting here innocently," says Jeremy, "thinking that I'm living my own life, celebrating the publication of a destined-to-be-obscure collection of stories, and suddenly I get reduced to the status of audience."

"You're perfectly free," says Rachel, "to ignore them."

"That's a self-conscious decision in itself. I don't want to *have* to ignore them."

"I was just talking to Sam this afternoon," says Blaine.

"So?" Jeremy demands. "Maybe you should go over and say hi. To your good friend *Sam*."

The arrival of my colleague Tina Christian at this moment seems a mixed blessing. Detaching herself from her own party, she immediately streaks over to our table and kisses me elaborately.

"Connor! I was just saying absolutely *everybody* comes here."

"And even a few nobodies," I say, before introducing her to my tablemates.

"Oh, you have such great taste," she says to Blaine. "You publish all my favorite books." This strikes me as a clever remark, seemingly diversionary as it is from the real focus of her interest.

"I'm just publishing Jeremy's," Blaine says—not news, obviously, to Tina.

"Oh, God, are you *that* Jeremy Green?" she burbles. "I just read the galleys of *Walled-In*."

"That makes you part of a very elite group," Jeremy says. "I think they only printed five or six."

"I thought it was brilliant."

Jeremy can't quite disguise his pleasure. We are all sluts of one sort or another.

"I can't stay, I'm with this group of losers," she says as she pulls up a chair beside me. "Unfortunately they're all my best friends."

VEGAN ACTIVISM

Tina seems to have more time than she imagined. After we have ordered, she tells Jeremy that she much prefers short stories to novels. "I mean, how many people have *time* to read novels?"

"Believe it or not," says Blaine, "there are a few of us left."

"Enjoying your charbroiled beef scab?" Jeremy asks the diner beside us, a young Wall Streeter who has been speculating about the size of his year-end bonus. Who, until moments ago, looked very satisfied with his lot, not least with his striped and succulent rib eye. Dining with Jeremy is always an adventure. Recently he was asked to leave an Italian restaurant on the Upper West Side after delivering a speech, from atop his chair, on the horrors of veal.

"Jeremy," says Blaine, "can't we, you know, just live and let live here? Do we *have* to make a scene?"

"Jeremy's always felt very strongly about this issue," counters Rachel, who has the prior claim on him and isn't about to relinquish it. "I don't think there's anything wrong with standing up for your principles."

"How does it feel," Jeremy asks Blaine, "to have an agent lecture you about principles?"

"Oh, *fine*, just because I try to look out for your interests, just because I try to beat up publishers for the best possible advance so that you can have the leisure to *write*—suddenly I'm *The Agent*."

Jeremy reaches over to embrace her. "It's true," he says. "Publishers come and go, but agents are forever."

Now Blaine's pissed, Rachel slightly mollified.

"Agents have feelings, too," says Tina, who would like, ever so much, to have one of her very own.

JEREMIAD

The appearance of a rottweiler outside the window on the sidewalk leads to the subject of Jeremy's beloved Sean. The negotiations have broken down entirely. "I offered three grand," he informs us.

"God," exclaims Tina, "what kind of dog *is* it?"

"Don't ask," says Rachel.

"*Please,*" adds Blaine, finally finding a point of concord with the agent.

"A toast to *Walled-In,*" Rachel says, raising her glass.

"Here, here," I say, raising my own.

"A book which," says Blaine, "I am as proud of as anything I have published in my entire career."

Jeremy raises his own glass. "A book which *Kirkus Reviews* has described as 'depressing and labored.' "

"*Kirkus* is a joke," says Blaine with Waspy hauteur.

"That's what the *New England Review* called my last collection," Jeremy recalls, " 'a joke.' "

"They did not," Rachel insists. "And anyway, whoever heard of the *New England Whatever.*"

"We just got a great blurb from Bret Ellis," says Blaine. "I meant to tell you."

"Oh, yeah, terrific," says Jeremy. "All the homicidal slackers will skateboard straight to Barnes and Noble for a copy of *Walled-In* and a latte."

"Not to mention," says Blaine, "the Auster and the Thom Jones quote."

"If I'm lucky somebody may think it's Tom Jones the singer. And fucking Auster had to write a movie before anyone got down on their knees."

"Let's not write off the audience for *Walled-In* just yet," Blaine says.

L I F E ,   P R O   A N D   C O N

Jeremy's malaise turns general. "Why did I come back this time? I wonder." A believer in reincarnation, he is referring to the mortal coil. "I mean, what was I thinking? Did I suddenly, in a weak moment, remember how good it feels to take a shower, the touch of warm water on the skin. Was that it?"

I can't help laughing. The literary posse glares at me.

Tina, on the other hand, tries to convince Jeremy to get high on life. "Don't you just want to see what happens next," she says. "I mean, I wake up every morning—well, noon, whatever—and it's a new day in the city, even when I'm hungover I basically can't wait to run out my door to find out what's out there—"

"A knife-wielding crackhead."

"I mean anything can happen—"

"Run over by a cab, raped and left for dead."

"Like when I was on my way here tonight, I had no idea I'd meet one of my favorite writers. . . ."

"Puh-lease," says Rachel, lifting her martini while I stare longingly at my empty glass.

"They look perfectly happy to me," says Tina, glancing over at Liam and Natasha. "Except I keep hearing he still has a sneaker for Julia."

Jeremy rolls his eyes. "I was definitely born in the wrong century," he says. "It all comes down to whether you live in the kind of universe where *DV* stands for 'Diana Vreeland' or 'Deo volente.' "

"Who's Deo Valente?" Tina asks.

Jeremy, through gritted teeth: "It means 'God willing,' in Latin."

"There *was* a Dino Valenti who was some kind of folksinger," Rachel chips in helpfully.

THE CRITIC

Looking up, I find myself looking at Kevin Shipley, who is glaring at our table, his general aspect if possible even more crabbed and dyspeptic than usual. Though I barely know him, he is someone of whom you feel compelled to ask: Have you ever used the word *joy?* Are you familiar with the definition? Although Tina tells me he actually has a cat on which he lavishes affection. I once applied for his job, before he had it, but of the several clips I submitted— freelanced reviews for obscure publications and Japanese to boot— two were positive. Which any reader of that mag could have told me was the wrong note entirely for a book review. As opposed to a celebrity profile.

I look to Tina, who seems to be *too* unaware of Kevin's scrutiny, her arm draped casually around the back of Jeremy's chair.

NOTHING WITH EYES

With the arrival of our meat-free appetizers—no one has dared to order animal protein, unless you count my linguine alla vongole— Jeremy is once again fiercely scowling at the next table, where the waveringly carnivorous investment banker is trying to finish his rib eye.

"Do you eat fish?" Tina asks Jeremy.

"Nothing with eyes," Jeremy snarls.

I am relieved to learn that my clams will escape censure.

"What if," Tina says, "we wear shades."

"That slab of flesh on Mr. Hermes' plate over there was grazing happily in a pasture just a few days ago."

This hardly seems the time to explain to Jeremy about the aging of beef.

"Excuse me," says the man's companion. "But I think you're incredibly rude." Suddenly she is up, standing beside our table in her Ralph Lauren suit and her black-velvet hairband, matching

Jeremy scowl for scowl. "You've been glaring at us, making me and my associate feel extremely self-conscious."

THE CASE AGAINST MEAT

"You know," says Jeremy, "quite aside from the cruelty and slaughter you're inflicting on the poor defenseless animals, there's also the far less important question of what you're doing to your own miserable bodies." Jeremy's voice expands to fill the dining room, which seems to be shrinking by the minute. "As a practicing carnivore, you can be certain that at this very moment some ten or fifteen pounds of undigested meat are lodged in your upper intestine, which might explain why you walk as if you had a Louisville Slugger three feet up your ass."

"Right on," Tina says. Then the woman takes a slap at Jeremy, her hand rebounding harmlessly from the ample mass of his hair. Even the luminaries at the front table who have so carefully avoided looking around the room can't help it at this point. Natasha, by the way, has very nice eyes.

"Typical blood lust," Jeremy sputters, as the captain rushes over to intervene. The woman's companion rises from his chair but seems at a loss as to his next move. "And *you*," says Jeremy, standing up himself and pointing at him, "you can just sit right back the fuck down unless you're looking for a Pellegrino high colonic."

The anal theme has become far too prevalent for my tastes.

RETREAT

Jeremy is finally persuaded by the captain and myself to wait outside while Blaine takes care of the check. Not before Tina slips him a card, in full view of Shipley, whom she has thus far failed to acknowledge.

From the sidewalk I watch as Rachel debates with herself whether or not to pay her respects to the high table. Fortunately for her, Jeremy is pacing farther up the street when she decides to risk it.

"Congratulations," Blaine says angrily when she joins us out-side. "You managed to upstage the movie stars. You must be very pleased with yourself."

"Did anybody ask for my autograph after I left?"

Rachel sighs. "Grow up, Jeremy."

United at last in their irritation with the author, the women announce they're sharing a cab to the Upper East Side.

"The only reason you're upset," Jeremy shouts after them, "is because you don't think I'm famous enough to be difficult."

"What say to a nightcap at Mount Olympus," I suggest as we watch the cab join a lazy school of its yellow brethren finning up Sixth Avenue.

"I think I've had just about enough merriment for one night."

The world, I think, is evenly divided between those who want company in their misery and those who fret alone. Though Jeremy would probably insist that it's divided between those who cherish principles and those who favor decorum.

MESSAGE FROM PHIL

"Hi, it's me. You there? . . . Guess you're out. I'm rushing. We're actually in Santa Barbara at the director's house and now I'm headed to L.A. I'm not sure about the schedule. It's nuts. Call you when I know where I am. Big kiss."

This message is on my machine when I return from dinner. It's the tone of voice that's so disturbing. A false, heightened breezi-ness. The words strung together on a thin wire of nervous gaiety.

CONNOR'S REACTION

These past few days he has been able to suppress his anxiety about Phil. But hearing her voice, he knows his suspicions were well founded. He *knows*. His ribs seem to constrict around his lungs, making him acutely aware of the throbbing muscle which is his heart. Panting like a winded dog, he paces the living room, slap-ping his fist into his palm.

Santa Barbara?

Maybe it's not too late. If he can reach her in L.A., maybe he can stop her from doing what it is he fears she has already done.

MODEL SEARCH

Dialing the Chateau Marmont, the Sunset Marquis, the Four Seasons, the Bel-Air, the Bel Age and the Peninsula while searching the drawers for cigarettes—which he gave up a year ago. He finally finds a pack of horrible stale Newports that someone left in the apartment. Lights one from the stove and suddenly thinks—Wait a minute, who smokes Newports? No one *he* knows. And Phil has never smoked. Jesus, she's been entertaining black guys in the apartment. No wait, could be a girl, one of her friends. But what friends? Who *are* her friends, anyway? Does she have any? Who the hell can he call?

Finally he calls her sort-of-friend Patty in Santa Monica, congratulating her on her infomercial, trying to sound casual as he asks if she has heard from Phil.

"You guys having, like, problems or something," she asks suspiciously. The tone of sisterhood closing ranks against the infidel male. Nothing like that, Connor assures her in a reedy, unconvincing voice. It's just that Phil's in L.A. and he's lost her number, the machine ate the tape, he needs to talk to her right away.

"I haven't talked to Philomena in six months."

"Yeah, well, if she does call, tell her to call me, okay?"

Who else can he call? He realizes how strange it is that his girlfriend should have so very few girlfriends of her own, a sign he should have noted before. Suddenly it seems irresponsible, even dangerous, to have so few friends. To have almost no friends. After all, who is your boyfriend supposed to call when he can't find you? At first this lack of comrades seemed attributable to their expatriation, later to their mutual romantic absorption in each other—back when they were fucking every day and he didn't much care if he ever got out of bed again. . . .

WOMEN BEWARE WOMEN

Connor remembers something Brooke once said: "Beware the woman who doesn't like other women; she's probably generalizing from her own character."

MODEL BEHAVIOR

Sometimes Phil would become friendly with another model; they would spring up like daffodils in our lives, briefly, their long legs sheathed in ripped jeans, long arms around their dark Euroboys . . . dinners at Raoul's and B Bar . . . *Bonsoir, there's Linda and Kyle . . . How was Milan? So sad about Richard and Cindy. Cristal and cigarettes, maybe just a little snort of H — where's Kate? More cigarettes! Buccal fat pads removed, plus her eyes . . . Actually, I almost never do coke anymore practically. . . .*

Generally these acquaintanceships would trail off, or end badly. "Whatever happened to Veronica," Connor would ask, only to be told that she turned out to be a real bitch. Not that he missed these brilliant nights as the dimbulb boyfriend, the awkward beauty accessory, the anonymous companion. *So nice to have met you, Collin. . . . What is it you do, Cullen? You must be very proud of Philomena, Curran. . . . What do you write, Kiran? Of course, you must know Court?*

FLASHBACK

"Why don't we ask Katrinka and her boyfriend for dinner?" you proposed one fine spring day.

"*You* ask them. The three of you can go out. Or better yet, just the two of you. You and Katrinka."

"I thought you liked Katrinka."

"I used to. Till I found out she was a liar."

"What did she lie about?"

"Lots of things."

"Like what?"

"Like she said you were coming on to her."

"She said that?"

"Uh-huh."

At this point you were hard-pressed to speak up in Katrinka's defense. In fact, it did seem she once might have flirted with you a little, and you felt guilty that you had not actively discouraged it, this flirting, partly because you were grateful to be noticed at all. You would have to watch that kind of thing—you vowed to make Philomena feel more secure. She would realize eventually that you loved her, and in the meantime it was just the two of you, you and Phil, dining à deux.

There are worse fates, of course, than finding yourself alone for the night with Philomena Briggs. At this moment you would gladly give up your own few friends for the privilege.

PANIC

The cigarette tastes so bad he immediately lights another.

On a flash of inspiration he rushes back to the bathroom and searches the cabinet beneath the sink, the drawers in the bedside table, her cosmetics case, the oval Shaker box and the shagreen jewelry box he bought for her twenty-sixth birthday. Lingerie drawer, scattering panties and bras to the winds. Under the bed, back to the bathroom, the soap dish in the shower, everywhere that he has ever seen her diaphragm. Which is not in the apartment. He slumps to the floor of the shower stall, still wet from his evening rinse.

She *knew* he would be at dinner with Jeremy when she called tonight. Oh, yes, definitely. The night she left, Connor asked if she would be home in time for Jeremy's big dinner. Phil wrote it in her book, said she'd try. This little detail, barely noticed at the time, now looming enormous. She fucking *knew*. Waited until he was out to call.

Santa Barbara?

As a last resort he checks his e-mail with all the optimism of a camel essaying the eye of a needle.

M O R E   F A N   M A I L

To: Scribbler@aol.com
From: Jenrod@inch.com
Subject: You are worthwhile!
Dear Connor:
It was GREAT to hear from you but I was totally amazed you sounded so DOWN on yourself. I think actually it is often the case that the best people are the hardest on them selves. How can you say your not a worthwhile person? LOOK AT YOURSELF! You are a successful writer for a national magazine!
    I think you have been listening to the wrong people. It's important to surround yourself with people who build U up not tear U down. Like me, sometimes I think I'm hanging out with the wrong people. All they think about is Thank God Its Friday and Look at that Guy in the BMW. I guess you would call us a gang. In high school I felt lucky to be part of it because you can't just be on your own but now that I am out with a job I want to better myself. Its hard when your with people who don't have any ambition except to be with the hottest guy which is maybe somebody who is doing something illegal for a living. Like my friend Tina she's really cool but last year she slashed this girl with a boxcutter who was supposedly stepping out with Jimmy Ortega and she had to have fifty eight stitches to her face. And sometimes she says I'm stuck up when really its just I want a better future. Anyway I better go. If my boss catches me on line I will be in big trouble.
    For what it's worth, I believe in you. REALLY! E me!
    P.S. Do you like to dance? Do you ever go to Chaos? Or even the Latin Quarter? Maybe we could meet sometime. How about Friday night? Me and Tina will be there at Chaos at midnight. See you there!

S U C C O R   F R O M   A   M O R E
C R E D I B L E   S O U R C E

Connor signs off, dials his sister. Perhaps she can convince him that his fears are groundless, say something to ease the incessant, throbbing pain.

For once in her life, Brooke picks up the phone.

"She's gone, Brooke."

"Yes, you told me. San Francisco, as I recall."

"She took her *diaphragm*, Brooke. Jesus, I can't stand it. I can't sit down. I can't stand still. I don't want to be in the apartment another minute but I don't want to leave in case she calls."

"Why don't you come over here?" Brooke proposes. "You can leave my number on your machine." Thankfully, she does not remind him, as is her wont, that there are people far worse off than he.

In the cab, shuddering uptown, he drums the back of the seat in time to his desperate heartbeat.

"What are you, Gene Krupa? Relax already." Last of the old New York cabbies.

When Connor sees his sister's face he comes apart like a three-dollar umbrella in a gale. Brooke scoops up the wrecked metal ribs and shredded black rayon and walks the whole mess inside. Half a dozen soothing, empty—make that false—formulae are uttered. *It's all right*, et cetera.

When he has partially regained his composure she is hefting a steaming kettle in the kitchen.

"I didn't know you knew how to boil water."

"You're thinking of Mom," she says. "I learned this in the lab. Actually, it's not as difficult as it looks."

"Just please don't say I'm better off without her."

"Only because it would arouse your chivalrous instincts. I long ago learned that the quickest way to get a guy panting for more abuse was to run down the lady in question. I have no desire to provoke you into defending her." Brooke looks uncharacteristically competent in an oversize Middlebury sweatshirt which Connor gave her about twelve years ago, with her hair swept back in a pony-tail, her thin, freckled hand with its striped scars resting on the kettle. If only he were allowed to fall in love with his sister. In fact, Phil thinks he *is* in love with Brooke. "Why don't you fuck your sister" being one of Philomena's late-night refrains. Connor has a sudden guilty insight: that his custodianship of Brooke has interfered with the care and feeding of his fragile girlfriend.

"Her *diaphragm*, Brooke."

"I thought you were the condom generation."

"I hate condoms. Swimming in a rain coat. Besides, we've been in a completely monogamous relationship for three years."

She raises her eyebrows at this doubtful assertion. "God, you smell like Lynchburg, Tennessee."

"I've been drinking."

"I'm *shocked*."

"It doesn't help."

"I wish you'd tell that to Dad."

"It just feels so goddamn bad."

"I know." Stroking his hip, she hands him a Beethoven mug full of steaming water on which floats a tea bag with pendant tag: Lapsang souchong. "What did you do, wet yourself?" she asks, removing her hand from his ass.

"I sat down in the shower."

"Let me get you a robe."

Connor slaps his hand against the wall. "I don't understand how she could be so eager to run off and fuck some other guy when I have to beg and plead just to get any once or twice a week."

"Shhh."

"It's not fair."

"I know."

FAIRNESS AND MATH

Brooke discovered injustice and the negative numbers on the same day. She was in Miss Tollitson's first-grade class at Winterhaven Elementary School, performing feats of arithmetic. Miss Tollitson was a fierce egalitarian of procrustean bent who felt that Brooke was a little big for her britches—Miss Smarty Pants, as she later complained to the principal. Brooke would have shined in any context, but nowhere quite so brightly as amongst the sons and daughters of intermarried dirt farmers, porch loungers and dead-machinery curators of Central Florida, from which stock Miss T herself was descended. One morning after Brooke had successfully answered an increasingly difficult series of additions and subtractions, Miss Tollitson snarled, "All right Miss McKnight, what's seven take away ten?" Arms folded high on her bony chest, a premature look of triumph (as Brooke tells it) suffusing her beaked, leathery visage. Of course, Brooke knew this was a trick question. But she was stubbornly determined not to be defeated by the old battle-ax. And suddenly, the answer seemed as obvious as if she had been Archimedes in his bath. She saw in her mind's bright eye a series of phantom integers, transparent abacus beads hovering in the void.

"Minus three," she announced.

Miss Tollitson's red-faced reaction verified her discovery. "We don't know about that yet," she sputtered. "That's sheer impertinence, Brooke McKnight. You just go right down to Mr. Brent's office and we'll see how smart you are."

And so Brooke was sent home from school for the crime of discovering the negative numbers before the Florida Board of Ed had planned for her to do so.

SUDDENLY, THE BUZZER

The door speaker crackles, announcing the arrival of Doug Halliwell, M.D.

"Oh, hell," says Brooke, smiling apologetically.

Possibly the last person in the world I would want to see at this moment.

"I'll get rid of him, I promise."

"I've been advising you to do that for months."

"*Please*, Connor."

"And don't you dare tell him my girlfriend has dumped me. I don't need his pity."

"Too late for that," Brooke mutters.

I retreat to the sofa to sulk, hoisting a copy of the *Mathematical Intelligencer* for a prop, hearing him at the door. . . .

"Just finished up at the, uh, hospital, and I thought you might, I don't know, want to get a bite, I mean we don't have to. Oh, I didn't . . . hello, Connor."

I wave absently in his direction, pretending to be absorbed in an article on knot theory.

"Connor and I are having a little family conference. But you're welcome to a cup of tea." I sneak a look in Brooke's direction in order to glare, but she's not about to let me catch her eye.

"I don't mean to . . ."

"No, no. That's all right."

I sense Mad Dog's presence at my back, hesitating to enter the room proper, standing politely in the foyer while Brooke rattles around in the kitchen. I can picture him, bobbing forward slightly from the waist, head deeply recessed into his shoulders, hair receding up his forehead. For some reason, his timidity offends me, though I'm not such a hardass as to snub him entirely. Perhaps it is my own timidity I see and dislike in his face, whose features I can never really remember from one meeting to the next.

But yes, that must be him, standing just as I imagined, in his khaki Sansabelt pants and his anorak. Now I remember what he looks like. With his forward-hunched posture, his bug eyes and Roman nose, he resembles a perched vulture.

"Have a seat," I suggest, as if I am the host, or the doctor.

He shrugs, moving tentatively into the room, examining its meager features. "How's the, uh, the writing going," he asks.

"I wouldn't know," I say. "You should ask the writers." His attempt to take my pretensions at face value further infuriates me. Dimly I perceive that Doug bears hardly any blame for the fact that I hate what I do for a living, and hate myself for what I have failed to do with my life, even as he returns from a sixteen-hour shift of plugging gunshot wounds and resurrecting gasping cardiacs. I know I'm behaving childishly—a glimmer of perception that only makes me meaner. It's seldom difficult to know how one *should* behave. The Golden Rule, the Categorical Imperative, all that. The former has been revised, of course: *Behave unto others as if they were about to become incredibly famous.*

THE DOCTOR'S VISIT

Brooke bustles in with a broken-handled mug, which Doug receives gratefully, grasping it as eagerly as if it were the answer, finally, to the nagging question of what to do with his hands outside of surgery . . . until he realizes how hot it is and searches frantically but quietly for a neutral surface on which to put it down.

"But you're still working for the, uh, the magazine, aren't you?" he persists, blowing on his scorched hands.

"Barely."

"How was your day, Doug?" Brooke chirps. I can't believe she perks up for this limp specimen.

"Not too bad." Thankfully he doesn't have to elaborate, being interrupted by his beeper.

"Use the phone in the bedroom," says Brooke, and then, as he disappears, she hisses: "Will you try for once not to behave like a total asshole, if only for my sake."

I'm stung. Me, an asshole? I remind her she said she was going to get rid of him.

Doug emerges to announce he's needed at the hospital. Someone at death's door. He seems relieved, actually, to be needed, to go back where he clearly belongs; God knows *I'm* relieved. He pauses just long enough to spill some tea down the front of his sweater. Brooke wipes him off and kisses him at the door.

"I don't understand what you see in that dork."

"He's sweet and kind and decent—three qualities nobody's going to pin on you. I've had a rotten year and I'm very grateful for Doug's interest."

"He has subzero personality."

"No, what he doesn't have is attitude. There's a difference."

I can't stand to see Brooke angry at me. We hardly ever disagree on anything, so I'm crushed by her failure to share my judgment of the good, the virtuous Dr. Halliwell. But I can see that she is mad, and to win her back I apologize. Knowing she wouldn't really appreciate the observation, knowing he can't probably help it, I won't even mention the funny way he wheezes instead of breathing.

A PARABLE

Later, sitting on the sleigh bed, Brooke strokes her brother's hair and, with another story from their childhood, his soul. A story about a Welsh terrier and a calico cat. "Remember old Rogue? How we could never get him to eat his dog food. Hated it. Tipped his bowl over and scattered food across the floor. But as soon as Clio stuck her whiskers in his bowl he'd go wild, barking and growling and running around in circles till she'd had her nibble. Then he'd rush in and devour every last bit of it."

Connor knows his sister too well not to take the point, but at the moment he is too unhappy either to acknowledge or dispute it.

"You've been with her three years. In all that time you've failed to demonstrate a commitment. But now that someone's got his nose in your bowl you're howling. I hate to say it, but this is kind of a guy thing. You boys think you want virgins, but I think what you really want is to put your peepees where the other peepees have been."

This somehow reminds me of the joke Philomena told in the cab en route to the Baby Doll Lounge the night before she left, and though it should be palliative it only makes me miss her all the more, thinking of the soft weight of her in my lap.

PHILOMENA'S JOKE

"So there's this guy," she begins, "—shut up and listen—this guy's shipwrecked on a desert island."

"Is this the one about the Doberman and the sheep?" asks Ralph, the hair genius.

"No it's not. Quiet!" She takes a whack at Ralph, and continues. "So this guy's wasting away on this desert island for weeks and months, till one day another big storm blows up, and another ship crashes on the reef. After a while he sees this body bobbing in the surf so he swims out and grabs this blond hair and pulls the body to shore. . . . *Quiet!* And it turns out to be Sharon Stone. Well, he gives her mouth to mouth—no, shut up. . . . He revives her and of course she's very grateful and all. No, she's *not* still naked, Connor, it doesn't matter. Okay fine she's naked. Anyway she's grateful and all but after a few weeks it's more than that. She realizes she's falling in love with the guy. And she's like, Isn't this great, if not for this shipwreck I never would've met the man of my dreams. Of course he's ecstatic—I mean, whoa, Sharon Stone's in love with him and he's in love with her and everything's great and they decide to get married if they ever get off this goddamn island but after a while she notices that he's getting moody, it's not quite the same. She tries to tell herself he'll get better but he just seems real depressed and finally she says, 'What's wrong? I'll do anything you want, just come back to me.' And he says it's nothing."

"Fag!" shouts Alonzo, self-described "powder fairy."

"Shut up, 'Lonz."

(And feeling Philomena in your lap, gazing at her close up, in profile, you felt painfully, irredeemably hetero.)

"But finally he says," she continues, " 'Will you really do anything I want?' and she goes, 'Of course,' so he says, 'I want you to dress up like a guy, there's like all these guys' clothes that've washed up on the beach—' "

"Told you!"

"Yes, I'm sure you can relate to that, 'Lonzo—and Sharon's

thinking, Shit, I knew it was too good to be true, he's getting all kinky on me, but she loves him so much she'll do it. And then he explains that after she gets dressed up he wants her to walk around one side of the island while he walks around the other side and they'll meet halfway. 'And when you see me, pretend you're some guy who knows me and ask me how it's going.' So she walks around one side, and when they meet she says, 'Hey, Frank, how's it going?' And he says: 'Going great man. You won't *believe* who I'm fucking. . . .' "

BACK TO THE PRESENT

"Why can't I just marry you?" Connor says.

"I make a bad wife. Just ask Jerry."

"Fuck Jerry. Jerry's a dickhead. Tell me another story. Please. Anything that doesn't involve slaughter and cruelty in other parts of the world."

ANOTHER STORY

"Have I ever told you about strategies of the hunt for large primes."

"Oh, God, not that one."

"As you know, primes are only divisible by themselves and one—they're like building materials of number theory, like fundamental particles in physics or the basic elements in chemistry. All the other whole numbers can be written as products of these primes. There are an infinite number of primes, of course, so you'd think it would be fairly simple to find them."

Undoubtedly, you would. But I'm betting . . . it's *not*.

"But actually it's quite tricky, even with the help of computers." As she speaks, I glance at the thin scars beneath the sleeve of her nightgown. "They behave very perversely and they're hidden among the other numbers in very unpredictable sequences. Searching for the really big ones—I'm talking numbers like two to the, say, seven thousand six hundred and thirteen power— searching for the big ones is kind of like trolling the surface of the ocean for giant marlin. You have to stake out a wide swath of territory and then kind of gradually close . . ."

This goes on for some time. Large primes aside, I'm wondering what the best strategy is for hunting petite models.

C O N N O R ' S   M I N D   W A N D E R S

Random thoughts:

A yearning for Philomena's body as site-specific as that of the salmon for the patch of watery gravel in which he was hatched. The belief that he will always miss her, that no one else will come so close to filling his intense, recurring need to swim upstream. That he will be like those poor anadromous finny pilgrims stuck in a pool at the base of a massive hydroelectric dam, forever exiled from home.

Is Brooke right? That the male of the species needs frequent verification of the desirability of the love or sex object? The only absolute proof being the consummation of interest on the part of another male, which consummation forever robs the lover of his sense of possession, and drives him completely insane with jealousy.

Is Connor guilty, as charged, of enjoying his model girlfriend's trophy status? Instead of encouraging her to do something that wouldn't make her so crazy? Instead of, for example, marrying her? Practically inviting her to escape into the arms of some horny photographer or male model or whoever may be ramming it up against her missing diaphragm at this very moment?

Or does his evasion of commitment reflect his aforementioned sense of his own unworthiness? Should he give her credit for admiring those few qualities that he values in himself: his intelligence, his impractical education and his lack of malice? Or does he, out of self-loathing, despise her for admiring in him such qualities as count for nothing in the marketplace?

SEXUAL SURROGACY DEBATED

"Do you think it's weird that when I have sex with Philomena I'm always conjuring up another sexual encounter."

Brooke thinks about it. "I suppose you could say it's like a stereoscope, one of those old optical devices, where you view photographs of the same object from two slightly different points of view, your two eyes putting together the images to create the illusion of depth."

"What exactly," you ask, "are the two eyes? In this case?"

"But a more sinister interpretation would be that you're incapable of appreciating the actual intimacy you enjoy with Philomena and you have to distance yourself from the domestic Philomena with whom you shop for groceries and pay the bills by turning her back into the kind of sex object who is displayed in Hollywood movies and glossy magazines like the one you work for, and in which she frequently appears. But if it makes you feel any better I think all men do that. Except that most of them have to leave their own apartment in order to supply the image."

JEEVES RALLIES ROUND

Connor still can't sit still. He paces around the living room, stopping to examine any domestic objects he fails to recognize. Finally, Brooke resorts to Wodehouse.

There is a tradition in the McKnight family of sojourning in Wodehouse territory when life seems especially grim and real. Connor appreciates the gesture all the more since Brooke doesn't believe that it is either possible or desirable to escape the sorrows and horrors of this world (although he once heard her bat around the concept of Possible Worlds in connection with some conundrum of logic).

She reads aloud about Bertie's attempts to steal the silver cow creamer from Sir Watkin Basset, while attempting to avoid matrimony with Basset's moony daughter Madeline. After more than an hour he suddenly feels exhausted from his ordeal and admits he might be able to sleep.

CONNOR'S DREAM

Your repose is tortured and storm tossed until Brooke finally takes you in her arms. All at once you feel nearly at peace. In the familiar warmth of your sister's embrace you feel you have arrived at your destination after a long, arduous, unhappy journey. You kiss your sister and drift off toward sleep, and in your dream you are embracing a beautiful woman. Could it be Pallas? It is not Philomena, certainly, but someone very familiar. You kiss her mouth and burrow into her chest. Watching yourself in your dream you feel radiant. And you are just on the verge of becoming whole when Brooke says, "No, Connor, don't. Connor, stop!"

ANOTHER DREAM

You are sitting in a pastoral field when Philomena suddenly drops down by your side, her eyes alight with lust. You have never seen this expression on her face, a wanton mask. She reaches for your jeans and unzips you. You ask her where she's been. "Can't talk with my mouth full," she says wickedly, bending down, proceeding to fill it. "What about all these people?" you ask prudishly, just noticing the presence of others. "I've already taken care of them," she says, looking up. And then you see that all the men around you are lying on their backs in postures of satiation with their jeans around their ankles. A man walks past, fixing his fly, and winks at you.

You wake in a panic, sit up. Brooke is breathing lightly beside you. What is peculiar about the dream: Philomena claimed to be too self-conscious to enjoy you going down on her, and out of some deeply misguided sense of mutuality felt that you, too, could do without.

In the dream you are as aroused as you are jealous, turgid with grief and lust.

BROOKE'S DREAM

Brooke dreams of bodies floating down a river in Tanzania, mutilated bodies cascading over the Rusumo Falls onto the rocks below.

AN ITEM IN THE <u>DAILY NEWS</u>

Grazing my morning tabloids on the E train, heading home, I come across this:

> . . . Highrise heartthrob LIAM NEESON at DA SILVANO, taking a swing at novelist JEREMY (*Walden*) GREEN, who was apparently paying too much attention to wife NATASHA RICHARDSON . . .

AD ON A BUS SHELTER

CLUB MED—LIFE AS IT SHOULD BE: White sand, turquoise water, caramel flesh. Thanks very much for reminding us. A cold drizzle falling here in Manhattan; a malevolent cloud has swallowed the tops of the Trade Center Towers.

JEREMY GREEN, LITERARY DETECTIVE

Upon returning home I rush to the answering machine. I checked once this morning from Brooke's, but that was forty minutes ago. Difficult as it was to leave the refuge of her nest, I thought my chances of hearing from Phil were better if I was stationed at the phone—although I left Brooke's number on the machine last night.

Only one call, from Jeremy. "Damnit, McKnight. Call me." Disappointed as I am to find his voice in lieu of Phil's, I call immediately. I'm always expecting some terrible message from Jeremy, or about Jeremy, who not only presents himself as a character in the second act of a tragedy, but also rewrites his will every six months:

currently I am his designated literary executor. As with my sister, my chief fear is that the third act may take place when I am out of sight.

"The *Times* review is running on Saturday."

"That's great." Apparently he hasn't seen the *News*. Far be it from me.

"How do you know it's great? Have you heard something?"

"I mean, just getting reviewed in the daily *Times* is kind of a big deal, isn't it?"

"Saturday is like going to Paris in August."

His call waiting clicks and he dumps me for Blaine.

Shortly he calls back. "I just reread *Goodbye, Columbus*," he informs me.

"Ah. Brenda Patimkin . . . underwater kissing . . . diaphragm." As soon as I've said it I feel the ache of loss and regret. *Diaphragm*—terrible word, obscene little Frisbees flashing across the edge of my vision, booby traps underlying the very path of my consciousness. I think that was the first time I heard of one, reading Roth's first novel. Had no idea what it was. Wish I still didn't.

"It's so *obvious*," Jeremy says indignantly. "It came to me like a goddamn lightbulb switching on over my head." More than a cliché, in Jeremy's case this sounds like a potential fire hazard. But I'm relieved, too, that he hasn't swallowed an entire bottle of Percocet, nor opened his veins in a warm tub after deciding that his talent—compared to the titans who were born of the sun who traveled a short while, et cetera—is too meager to justify his continued consumption of planetary oxygen.

"Salinger," he announces, cryptically. "Roth took Salinger's suppression of his own Jewishness, the phantom Jewishness of Salinger's faux Wasp characters, and made the subject matter explicitly Jewish. The social observation, the class consciousness, the hyperrealistic observation of the courtship rituals of postwar urban youth—and then he used the license that Bellow and Malamud had granted to speak explicitly of Jewish themes. Voilà— *Goodbye, Columbus*."

"The Glass family *was* Jewish, weren't they?"

"Half Irish, half Jewish," Jeremy says impatiently. "The faith passes through the mother, in this case Bessie, who's Irish. So, no. Salinger was probably unconsciously trying to cop some Irish-lit cred. But Roth—I mean, sure, *Goodbye, Columbus* is fucking great. I'm just saying it doesn't come out of nowhere."

"That's a relief," I say. "Now, how about a drink? A restorative . . . *cocktail?*"

"I've got my shrink in half an hour."

"Ah yes, the Celtic and the Hebraic approaches to sorrow and confusion, respectively."

"I need more meds to get through this fucking publication."

"Send me the book," I say in parting.

E - M A I L

To: Scribbler@aol.com
From: Jenrod@inch.com
Subject: Waiting on U
My friend Tina thinks I should send you a photo so you won't think I'm "a dog." You shouldn't judge a book by its cover I always say but let's face it in this business Plain Janes aren't exactly the flavor of the month except maybe Kathy Bates, no disrespect intended I think she's a major talent. I am sending U my "head shot" by "snail mail" which actually shows more than just my head. E me! I'm waiting with baited breath.

PREEMPTIVE STROKE

Monday: We're lunching with Pallas. Of course, we had to promise her a hundred dollars for her time. Plus the lunch. Why are we doing this? Trying, perhaps, in case it becomes necessary, to implement the plan called Life After Philomena? Just to assure ourselves of our essential fidelity we beat off before leaving the apartment, conjuring up a particularly juicy episode in which Philomena set aside her distaste for oral sex.

PALLAS BY DAY

Pallas arrives just a few minutes late. Conversation in the restaurant falls and finally rises again, a collective susurration. She is discreetly breathtaking in a white T-shirt (but of course!) and a simple blue silk jacket with matching trousers. Is it just my imagination, my insider's knowledge of her unclothed form, or is there a fine, invigorating tension between her natural abundance and the architectural strictures of the tailored suit? Or, then again, is it possible she actually looks kind of silly in clothes? I rise and hold her chair, brushing against her arm, inhaling an aggressive perfume.

"What do you know?" she asks.

"Less and less, Pallas. I'm in an epistemological recession."

"Do other people understand half the junk you say?" She doesn't seem worried, just mildly curious, head swiveling around the room. "Where are the celebrities," she asks. Apparently I'd promised her some.

Quick scan of the room. Somehow I doubt that the editor in chief at Farrar, Straus & Giroux qualifies in Pallas's book. So I decide to go on the offensive. "In what way would it improve your life if there *were*, say, a movie star in the room?"

"What?"

"Did you know that until relatively recently, historically speaking, actors were viewed as occupying a lower position on the great chain of being than, say, tapeworms or silverfish? They were viewed—and this is pretty hard to dispute when you think about it—as pretenders, poseurs, dissemblers; their moral character therefore highly suspect. I mean what explains this fucking international epidemic of thinking that people who are paid to simulate real life on-screen are somehow more *real* than the rest of us. We're suffering from a mass hysteria, an epidemic of surrogacy, vicariously living the lives of Pamela Anderson and Charlie Sheen."

Disinclined to lubricate the flow of conversation, Pallas seems to be searching the room again.

"So," I ask, "do you like your job?" A desperate conversational gambit.

After squinting for a long moment at a distant diner who turns out not to be famous, she glances back to me and shrugs her shoulders, thereby animating her chest in a mesmerizing manner. "Yeah, it's okay. It's kind of fun, I guess. The money's pretty great." She taps at the pack of Seven Stars I have absently removed from my pocket. "Hey, I didn't know you smoked. All the Japs at the club smoke that brand. We grow tobacco down where I'm from. Smokeless mostly. That was probably one of the reasons I left. Every time you make out with some stud you stick your tongue in the stuff. You'd reach down for a Coke or a brew and find yourself swigging some guy's spit."

Amazing—we are practically having a conversation. This is the longest speech I've ever heard from Pallas, replete with intimate glimpses of her past.

"What do you want to do with your life now that you're here," I ask cautiously. "I mean, you can't keep dancing forever."

"I want to be an actress."

"Ah, knock me over with a feather."

"How come you're so mean about actors?"

"Probably just jealous," I say.

"You should come to my acting class."

I wave to the waiter, who is surely in somebody's acting class, and point to my empty glass of Stoli Cristall.

"I think dancing's great training, you know, appearing before an audience and all, and it definitely helps with your inhibitions and all."

"Which inhibitions might those be, Pallas?"

"Do you know John Cusack?" she asks.

"Not personally. Why?"

"I was just thinking that guy over there kind of looks like him. A little."

"Have you heard from Chip Ralston?"

"Is that why you asked me to lunch?"

"I asked you to lunch because I'm tragically infatuated with you." Which is, oddly, somehow true, despite the fact that I'm even more desperately in love with Philomena than ever now that she has dumped me, despite the fact that everything that comes out of Pallas's mouth is a cliché or worse. This kind of love I could never explain to my sister.

"Somebody called from his manager's office. They made a date for dinner next week."

"Chip's manager's taking you out?"

"No, you dope. *Chip's* taking me out to dinner."

"I don't suppose you might tell me *where* Chip's feting you?"

"Actually, I don't know. Someone is going to call me that day and tell me."

The waiter comes over and recites the daily specials—all of which sound vaguely nauseating.

"How about a cocktail?" I suggest.

ONE OF MOM'S FAVORITE WORDS

Cocktail. One of the earliest of words I learned at my mother's breast. (In fact, had my mother breast-fed me I would have undoubtedly imbibed them with her milk.) *Shall we have a cocktail? . . . I think it's almost cocktail time.* I'd have my juice and she'd have hers, from which I was allowed a sip. And, afterward, the sweet-sour smell of her wet kisses and the sound of her laughter, like ice in a silver shaker. Whereas my father's word was *highball. I think I'll build myself another highball.* A word I'm less fond of, evocative as it is of masculine bluster, disputations and broken glassware. Then, once he'd built himself a highball and consumed it, he would pay himself a *dividend.* (This economic model seems to have fucked up my sense of capital formation and my chance of being an investment banker—the operative concept being that you got rewarded for consuming.)

Later in life, the word *cocktail* betokened a perpetual silvery Manhattan dusk when the night with its lurid promise was all ahead of you. A portmanteau of sorts, a sum of parts, a word which seems to compound the two instruments of the sex act, as practiced by heteros. . . . This thought turning rancid as I imagine Philomena splayed and impaled . . . and then I recall last night's dream. . . .

Pallas orders a kir royale. I am drinking heavily, self-consciously, though it apparently has no effect whatsoever.

A WAVE OF SADNESS

"Why should I tell you about Chip," Pallas pouts. "You could be, like, one of those stalkers."

"I'm not crazy," I say. "I'm just . . . sad. I think my girlfriend's run off with someone else." I hadn't really intended to tell Pallas, and I was not consciously trolling for sympathy. Though I am gratified when she takes my hand and looks directly into my eyes for what may be the first time in our brief association.

"Poor, baby," she goes.

"I deserve it."

"She'll be back."

"I don't think so, Pallas." I haven't actually realized that I believe this until I hear myself say it. I turn away from Pallas's benign gaze, the lurid dream-image of Philomena poisoning the air around me.

"Well, don't let any grass grow under your feet." She reaches over and strokes my cheek.

"I can't blame her. I mean, look at me. Having lunch with you, for instance. I mean, no offense, but."

"You're actually a pretty nice guy. Don't beat yourself up. You never really even hit on me. Not really. I mean, do you have any idea how rare that is? You wouldn't believe what I have to put up with every night."

"Don't mistake timidity for virtue. Would you excuse me for a minute?" Overcome with a sudden wave of grief, I lurch downstairs to the phone, where I dial my machine and check my messages.

Despite or even because of my appreciation of the luminous Pallas, all of Philomena's virtues have come crowding back to claim my doting attention. The way she never returned from a trip without bringing me a present, for instance: a belt from Milan, a fucking beret from Paris, a pair of shades from L.A., an antique globe from the Upper East Side. The way she hid little notes in my luggage when I traveled. *Imagine me with you right now doing nasties all over your body.* Our first trip on ecstasy. Her childlike devotion to the rituals of Christmas. The fact that it was *possible* to have an interesting conversation with her, unlike certain other parties one might imagine oneself to be in love with, and despite the howling mindlessness of her so-called profession—certainly no more banal than my own.

TEMPORARY RELIEF

One message—from Jillian Crowe's office, asking me to call in immediately. Then, a hand on my shoulder—Pallas behind me, looking compassionate, concerned.

"You're crying," she says.

"I am?" She opens the door to the bathroom, which in fact is not equipped with a bath. "That's the men's," I say, as she peeks in. She nods, takes my hand and hauls me in behind her. She removes a Kleenex from her purse and wipes my eyes. Then she kisses me on the forehead. At which point I really fall apart. She embraces me, folding me into her soft contours, rubbing her hand across my back. "There, there . . . whoa, what's this? *Somebody's* feeling better."

Kissing my neck as her hands search for my fly, and then for the opening in my boxer shorts and then, Oh, God, as in: There is a . . . oh yes. I shouldn't be doing this—though I'm not really doing much of anything except submitting to the delicious friction. But it is already too late to contemplate resistance to the insistent rhythm of Pallas's ardent hand. . . . She releases me only long enough to (insert audible moan of pleasure here) lick her hand. And as she sets to her task it occurs to me that in sex, as in life, there is a delicate—and, in the current case, exquisite—balance between lubrication and friction. Facilitation and resistance.

"Pallas, *please.*" Apparently this is my voice, with its urgent note of entreaty—though I am not sure what I'm begging for. More? Or perhaps I am asking her to promise that this flood of ecstatic sensation will never cease, or at least that the pain will not rush in again once it subsides. In any case, Pallas gently nibbles at my lips as her hands work their thorough wonders. I suspect she's had some practice. In fact she does it better than I do it myself.

But here's the really weird thing, as Pallas—God bless her—sinks to her knees: from that moment till the end, I am fantasizing about Philomena.

"Thank you thank you thank you," I groan, as Pallas spits discreetly into the sink and washes her hands.

"You needed that," she explains plausibly.

POSTORGASMIC DEPRESSION

Still thinking of Philomena, missing her more than ever as I hold the men's room door open for Pallas. And for a moment I hardly register the striking fact that Jillian Crowe is standing by the phone outside, very minimal and forbidding in a dark gray, probably Calvin Klein, suit, thirty blocks south of her usual lunchtime post at the Royalton. I am reminded of what someone once said about her: that she could have been beautiful if she hadn't decided to be elegant instead. Her eyebrows rise above the tortoise rims of her shades as she registers me and my companion. Unfortunately the pay phone is situated in such a way that it is difficult to squeeze past even someone as svelte as Jillian Crowe.

"I'll call back," she barks into the receiver. "*You* I've been looking for," she says to me.

I shrug. "Busy busy busy."

"Yes, I can see that."

"This is, uh, Pallas . . ." The Christian name, pagan as it is, hangs suspended in the air on a gust of rising intonation, for I realize I've never known her surname. "Pallas, Jillian Crowe." Jillian regards Pallas with that special condescension that thin women who look good in clothes reserve for voluptuous women who look best without them.

Turning to me, Jillian asks, "Where *exactly* do we stand on the Ralston piece?"

"I'm, well, still working on it."

"Ah, you two were discussing the article in the men's room, were you?"

"Chip?" Pallas inquires brightly. "We were just talking about him."

A sudden, stupid inspiration: "Pallas is Chip's girlfriend."

This has the desired effect on Jillian, who looks at Pallas with new regard, and Pallas seems to take it in stride, raising her shoulders. Jillian scrutinizes her more closely, as if remembering her dimly from another life and trying to figure out which one. "Weren't you at the Metropolitan Art Society benefit with Charlie Lapidus?"

Pallas shrugs. "I don't really recall."

This seems like a good time to leave. I slide past Jillian, towing Pallas, waving enthusiastically on my way up the stairs.

"Ralston by the end of the week, Connor."

"Ah, yes, well . . ." I dismiss her with a jaded flutter of my hand; somehow I have nearly convinced myself that the Ralston piece is well and truly under way.

Pallas for her part swans back to our table with the haughty bearing of a movie star's consort; upon resuming her seat she adopts the self-consciously oblivious celebrity mien, refraining from looking out around the room in order to avoid meeting the tedious stares of idolaters. She does it well, I must say. Even her manner with the waiter has a new callow intimacy. Laughing louder than necessary at my inane attempts to amuse her, she devours her steak while I ventilate my soft-shell crabs with my fork; how, I wonder, could I have failed to notice before now how much these crustaceans resemble the giant, unkillable water bugs that climb out of the drains in my apartment? Stabbing them again for good measure.

Later, I steer Pallas past Jillian's table and put her in a cab. "You're an angel of mercy," I say.

"You're sweet," she says absently, already gone, our adventure in the men's room ancient history for her, as she contemplates her future with Chip: the trips to Cannes, the Academy Awards, the pesky tabloid allegations.

H O M E

I've been robbed. This is my first thought when I return to the apartment. The place is trashed, the contents of drawers and cabinets strewn across the floor and countertops. Or else my search for cigarettes and Philomena's diaphragm was more thorough than I realized.

No messages. One e-mail.

To: Scribbler@aol.com
From: Jenrod@inch.com
Subject: Photo
Dear Connor:
God I am *so* embarrassed, I shouldn't have sent you that picture but Tina talked me into it. It's like last year when she told us we had to beat down this girl she didn't like, I didn't want to but I did. Plus we'd been drinking and smoking and I wasn't really thinking too straight. If you haven't looked at it yet please don't, gotta go here comes my supervisor. . . .

T R U A N T   S I S T E R

A call from Brooke's psychopharmacologist:

"I'm sorry to bother you, Mr. McKnight, but I was a little concerned about your, ah, well, your sister. She's missed her last two appointments and she's not answering, that is to say she's not returning, my phone calls."

"I saw her last night," I say. "She seemed . . . okay."

"Ah," he says. "Well, I wonder if."

"You want me to have her call you?"

"Well . . ."

"Doctor, exactly how would you diagnose my sister's . . . problems."

"Well, I wouldn't want to, that is to say, there's no simple explanation. I would say that she manifests a complex of symptoms that I wouldn't want to—"

"Jesus Christ, Doctor. Is she clinically depressed? Would you say that? *Can* you say that?"

"She exhibits symptoms of depression, but I really can't . . . this falls in the area of doctor-patient—"

I hang up on the off chance that Philomena might be trying to call.

A CALL FROM MOM

"Hi, honey. How's every little thing with you?"

"Swell," I say. Mom has such a dreamy and ethereal disposition that I try never to puncture the bubble. The last, miraculous child of ancient parents, she grew up in an atmosphere of benign and privileged neglect in Charleston, then wafted through Bennington, till my father brought her to ground, briefly, after a mixer at Williams. When Dad graduated a few months later, they married and moved into my grandfather's house in Florida, where Mom resumed the life of her childhood—painting landscapes, tending the garden and riding. One hates to worry her. When Jeremy met her he declared that she was on her final incarnation, a nearly complete being making the final trip to earth.

"You sound tired," she says. "Are you all right, sweetie?"

"Just fine, Mom."

"I don't know how you do it," she says, "I swear you're going to work yourself to death up there."

"I'm okay."

"Your father sends his love. Is there anything I can bring you?" The annual Manhattan pilgrimage commences in a few days. I can't think of anything I want from Central Florida, except perhaps a sinkhole in which to disappear.

"Just your own sweet self," I say.

M A I L

Amidst the bills and magazines a letter for Philomena Briggs, addressed in handwritten block letters. No return address. The envelope, which has no watermark, is cheap enough that I can by holding it up to the light see a handwritten letter within, though unfortunately I can't really read it without tearing the envelope open. Which is the work of a moment.

> Dear Bitch:
> You think im a no body but well see about that. God made you pretty but I can make you ugly.

C O N N O R   T O   T H E   R E S C U E

Connor calls Philomena's booker, exhilarated by his legitimate fear for Phil's well-being.

"Liz, it's Connor. I've got to —"

"Sorry, Connor. Even if I knew where she was I couldn't tell you."

"She's in danger."

"Is that a threat?"

"There's a letter here from some nutcase —"

"Opening her mail, are we?"

"This guy knows where we live."

"Where *you* live."

"Jesus, Liz. I'm worried for her."

"If I hear from her I'll pass that on."

"But what about the letter?"

"All the girls get these things. What planet have you been on? If you send it along I'll put it in Phil's file."

"Please, Liz . . ."

"Goodbye Connor."

A S U M M O N S

Call waiting clicks; Jillian Crowe's assistant is on the other line. "Jillian wondered if you would be available this evening to escort her to a dinner at the home of Christina Carlton and Jason Lentz."

Apparently my stock is up since I emerged from a restaurant men's room with Chip Ralston's alleged girlfriend on my arm and a shit-eating grin on my face. Christina Carlton is, of course, an actress: I once interviewed her, shortly before she married a music mogul.

"Jillian will be sending a car. Also an outfit."

"What, it's a costume party?"

"We have you down as forty regular. What size shoes do you wear?"

S A R T O R I A L A I D

At seven-fifteen the town car arrives, glistening with sleety rain. The driver, a taciturn Irishman, hands me a garment bag and tells me he'll wait in the car. At least she didn't send someone to dress me.

I emerge stylishly from my apartment in my John Bartlett suit with navy-on-navy shirt-and-tie ensemble.

We drive uptown to pick up Jillian at her building off Madison. The doorman calls her while I stand in the lobby admiring the neoclassical architectural prints.

"You look wonderful," I say, admiring her tight, lime-green pants and black turtleneck.

She examines me, loosens my tie, shakes her head. "Lose the tie," she advises. "Always underdress a little, if only to make others worry that they're overdressed."

Satisfied, she takes my arm. "Anyway, we're going to the *West* Side."

BACKGROUND, SHALLOW AND DEEP

"They tried to get into 740 Park," Jillian informs me of our host and hostess. "Probably the best building in New York. Although the really secure residents use the other address, 71 East Seventy-first, which is the other entrance. But the board turned them down. I mean, what were they thinking? What was their Realtor thinking? Showbiz? CPW. A building like *that* doesn't want *show* folk. . . ."

"It's nice to know," I observe, "that there are still standards, somewhere."

She smiles, the first time in many moons that I have earned her approbation. "So tell me about your rest-room assignation. I'm quite impressed. Too bad you can't use it, it would make quite a nice little set piece: intrepid reporter emerging from the loo after a quickie with the oblivious star's concubine. Sad that we have such a morally upright editorial stance."

"Is that the stance where we try to convince young women to obsess about their appearance and weight while spending thousands of dollars on the clothing manufactured by our advertisers?"

"Is that supposed to be an original observation? Don't try to be cynical. You don't do it very well."

POLITE CONVERSATION AT THE MAJESTIC

Jillian presents me to our hostess, Christina Carlton, a woman with extensive Broadway and Hollywood background who used to play sexpots but now is trying, reluctantly, to make the transition to playing somebody's mother. In the meantime marrying Jason Lentz, one of the many gentlemen who became rich by getting fired from one of Time Warner's music labels. Fortunately, surprisingly, she is pleased to see me.

"Oh, I remember you," she trills in a voice piercing enough to halt ancillary conversation. "I was so delighted with that lovely article you wrote, and I told my manager I wanted to do something nice for you, and he said, 'Well, darling, I'm sure he'd appreciate a nice blow job.' "

The room finds this a hoot, but what's more entertaining, I discover, is my reaction, exacerbated, perhaps, by the fact of Christina's suggestively puffed, chipmunk cheeks.

"Oh, look, he's blushing. He's actually blushing."

"I didn't know anyone knew *how* to blush anymore."

This remarkable talent of mine for showing embarrassment is remarked upon as I am introduced to the other guests, including my host, looking very much at home in jeans and a cashmere sweater; James Croydon, the editor of *Beau Monde*, in full Savile Row armor, who appears to be doing a Tom Wolfe imitation; and Todd Fulham, the decorator, in basic downtown black, who tells me he did the apartment, a ten-million-dollar penthouse disguised as an Adirondack hunting lodge. He takes me on a brief tour, pointing out the signed Stickley, the William Morris daybed, the Frida Kahlo canvas, the Hopi and Marblehead pottery. In the library, he hands me his business card on which he has also written his home number with the invocation *Anytime!*

"I'm afraid," I say, "that your talents far exceed my decorating needs."

"It's not your apartment I'm interested in."

"Well, I can't tell you how sorry I am to admit that I'm one of those poor bastards who's helplessly drawn to the opposite sex."

"Oh, come on," he says. "You're walking Jillian, you work for a fashion magazine for God's sake. Don't play straight with me." He strokes the sleeve of my borrowed suit as if to underline his point.

"Appearances can be deceiving."

"And deceit can be so appealing. Are you sure you're not just teasing me?" he says, as a liveried servant enters and announces dinner.

F A U X   P A S

At the table I discover myself seated between Anne Sheridan, the designer, and a voluptuous young blonde whom I'm nearly certain I recognize as a dancer at Mount Olympus. She is the escort of Charles Lapidus, the grinch who owns airlines and cosmetics companies and a movie studio, and like me she is clearly out of place at this glossy gathering. She tells me she is a law student at NYU. When I ask her if by any chance we've met before she says coldly, "I don't think so," and ignores me for the rest of the evening. Anne Sheridan compliments me on my John Bartlett suit, and between courses remarks to our hostess: "Now, Christina, keep your head above the table at all times." Everyone else seems to get the joke before I do. Blow jobs seeming to be today's leitmotif. "Look," Anne says, "he's blushing again."

I try to keep a low profile, which is fairly easy, since the topics of chat are foreign to me, until the table starts in on the O. J. Simpson civil trial.

"Can you believe Don Ohlmeyer is still friends with O.J.?"

"He actually believes he didn't do it."

"Oh, *come* now. The man isn't stupid."

"O.J. or Don?"

"Take your pick."

"I'd rather not, actually."

"And now he denies he ever beat her."

"There ought," I say, "to be a special circle of hell reserved for any man who beats a woman." For some reason this comment seems to freeze the conversation. If I'd thought the sentiment was in any way controversial I would not have expressed it. But those few people who bother to glance at me do so as if I have just advocated some particularly egregious form of child molestation.

Finally our hostess breaks the silence: "Can you believe," she asks, "that Whoopi Goldberg actually got past the co-op board in the Forman's building?"

IN THE CAR, ON THE WAY HOME

"Was that your idea of a joke or were you *trying* to wreck the evening?" Jillian asks as soon as the driver closes the door behind her. "Don't tell me you didn't know that Charles Lapidus beat the shit out of Samantha, his ex-wife. I mean, you would have had to be living on the moon not to know that."

"So *that's* why no one would look at me for the last hour."

"It was in every column in the city. My God. It's not exactly like I can call him tomorrow and apologize. And what did you say to his date to offend her?"

"I think she was upset that I'd seen her naked."

"You really are hopeless," Jillian says. "What ever inspired me . . . God, I'm so tense." She cocks her head from side to side, then slides over beside me. "Are you any good with your *hands*, at least? Make yourself useful and get this crick out of my neck." She turns in the seat, presenting me with her back.

As I tentatively knead her neck, she says, "Surely you can do a little better than that." I dig in. For all its outward grace and Nefertitian extension, her neck is as gnarled to the touch as an Alpine conifer clinging to a wind-scoured cliff. Philomena's neck would get this way; in order to facilitate the present task I pretend I'm unknotting her after a hard day in front of the cameras.

"I see your female fans are sending you dirty pictures."

"Beg your pardon?"

"There was a photograph going around the office today. Part of this morning's reader mail. Hardly suitable for publication. I must say you seem to be a very popular boy lately. I'm beginning to think you possess hidden talents." She places a hand behind my head and pulls me toward her; suddenly her tongue is probing my mouth like a plumber's snake.

"This is kind of awkward for me," I say when she finally releases my head and reaches for my belt.

"Worried about your girlfriend?"

"I'm not even sure," I say, "that I *have* a girlfriend."

She looks at me aghast. "What do you mean?"

"She's kind of missing at the moment."

"But she's coming back?"

I shrug. "I'd like to think so."

"God," she says, drawing herself away. "I didn't realize you were unattached."

"Is that . . . a problem?"

"I never fuck unattached men."

Not a moment too soon, we have arrived in front of Jillian's building.

"Don't bother, I can walk myself to the door. The driver will take you wherever you want to go." She kisses me on the cheek, her lips chapped as sandpaper, while the driver holds the door.

"If your girlfriend comes back, you can consider my offer open. And if she doesn't, well . . . I'm sorry."

The door closes. Jillian starts to walk to her door, turns and walks back to tap on the window, which I lower. "Next time you're shopping for steady companionship, I would advise you to avoid the narcissistic professions."

A TYPICAL MORNING
IN THE WEST VILLAGE

10 a.m. Wake. Headache. Remember that Philomena has abandoned you, and is probably waking up with someone else. Someone who in the first flush of new love gets to fuck her in the morning, as you once did.

Heartache. Back to sleep.

11:15 a.m. Waking again. Realize that Philomena is still gone. That some nutcase is out there stalking her. That he has obviously written to her before, yet she never even mentioned it to you. What else didn't she tell you?

Guilt-ridden at sleeping so late, you crawl out of bed and survey disorderly, depraved bedroomscape: shoes, socks, jeans, 'zines, empty Evian and Absolut bottles. Vow to clean up bedroom. Soon.

For sure. Search top bureau drawer for the nude photo of Philomena that she gave you two years ago for Valentine's Day, for purposes of tormenting yourself, and possibly purposes of masturbation. Fail to find it. It, too, is gone. Consider what this means.

Could she have taken it back? Add this to your list of damning clues, along with her unpaid half of the rent and the missing diaphragm.

F U R T H E R   C O R R E S P O N D E N C E

To: Scribbler
From: Lawgirl
Subject: Brooke

Bro:

Finally talked to Brooke which did little to ease my mind. Jesus, I feel bad about man's inhumanity to man, but not fulltime. Is she still seeing her shrink? Can't you take her out to see a movie, or something? She's not cutting herself, is she? Sorry about your girlfriend. Next time, try Black. You'll never go back.

R E A L   L I F E

11:20 a.m. Shower. No shampoo. Mental note: Buy some. File it next to yesterday's identical mental note. By this time your mind is as messy with untended business as your apartment.

11:45 a.m. Newsstand for the *Times* and the *Post*. The former because you're a serious guy and the latter because you're not.

11:48 a.m.–12:30 p.m. Acropolis Coffee Shop, consuming coffee, bagel and newsprint. Refugees in Zaire. Anna Nicole Smith redundantly in a coma. Whitney threatens to dump Bobby Brown unless he goes to the Betty Ford Clinic. A gang of schoolgirls in Queens slashing the face of one of their classmates with a boxcutter.

You look up at the framed photograph of Philomena, right

between the big-haired soap star and Matthew Broderick. *Best to all the gang at the Acropolis.*

But what about me, Phil? What wishes for me?

Here in the far West Village, the midday coffee shop clientele is thankfully weighted in favor of goggle-eyed fast-breakers with pillow-pressed coifs sucking down coffee and staring suspiciously at their bagels, although there are a few early rising working folks tucking into their second meal of the day, devouring hamburgers and tuna melts. On the way out, a lingering look at the icon on the wall, your lost love smiling down on her public. *Best to all the gang.* . . .

12:48 p.m.—Safe at home, you sit at your desk examining mail, which comes complete with requests for money. Should you give to the Gay Men's Health Crisis, Amnesty International, your alma mater? *"Mr. McKnight,* won't you consider a gift of $1000 or more?" You would like to, but your bank statement shows some seven hundred less than that in your checking account. The phone and electric bills should certainly be paid. *Someone* ought to do that, some philanthropist perhaps, like that guy who died recently who used to award trust funds to injured cops and mugging victims. Second notice from the phone company, already ten days overdue. Picking up the receiver, you still get a dial tone! If only you could find your checkbook underneath all this paper. Here's something—a letter you received about two weeks ago:

CHAIN LETTER

With Love All Things Are Possible

This paper has been sent to you for good luck. The original is in New England. It has been around the world nine times. The luck has been sent to you. You will receive good luck within four days of receiving this letter provided you send it on. This is no joke. You will receive good luck in the mail.

Send no money, send copies to people you think need good luck. Do not send money, faith has no price.

Do not keep this letter. It must leave your hands within 96 hours. An RAF officer received $470,000. Jon Eliot received $40,000 and lost it because he broke the chain. While in the Philippines, George Hish lost his wife 51 days after receiving the letter. He had failed to circulate the letter. However, before her death he had received $7,775,000.00.

Please send 20 copies and see what happens in four days. The chain comes from Venezuela and was written by Saint Anthony DeCrou, a missionary from South America. Since this copy must tour the world, you must make 20 copies and send them to friends and associates. After a few days you will get a surprise. This is true even if you are not superstitious. Do note the following: Constantine Dias received the chain in 1953. He asked his secretary to make 20 copies and send them. A few days later he won the lottery of two million dollars.

Dolan Fairchild received the letter and not believing, he threw the letter away. Nine days later he died.

Do not ignore this. It works.

Here perhaps is the source of your calamity and subsequent grief: like the hapless RAF officer you broke the chain. What if you had made twenty copies and mailed them out? *If only* . . . In your bereaved state this shrill imperative improbably strikes home; you are even prepared to believe in the omniscient narrator who has followed the exfoliation of this letter from Venezuela out across the planet, the last omniscient narrator on the planet, the others having retired or been fired from the good novelistic jobs, leaving this one poor slob to become a kind of ethereal gumshoe, a semiliterate detective shadowing the myriad incarnations of this barely grammatical letter into the office of Jon Eliot and the bedroom of Dolan Fairchild and up the brain stem of George Hish (which names, I might add, seem to me like the lumpy fabrications of an undergraduate creative writer) and on through your own mail slot into the hallway where you have planted your desk.

Oh, to be a character in an old-fashioned story. Or a big-budget romantic comedy, since Hollywood has taken over from novelists the business of wish fulfillment: Mixup unmixed, discord morphing to concord, misunderstanding understood. FADE TO: kiss.

In your pathetic, tenderized state you are almost prepared to believe in a capricious and personalized fate to which this innocent-looking piece of Xerox paper is attached as if by a rheostat. *Connor McKnight left the letter sitting on his desk. A week after receiving it his girlfriend packed up her diaphragm and disappeared. Two weeks later he was run over by a taxicab.* Maybe it's not too late. Maybe if you sent it out now. . . .

Looking for some business-sized envelopes in which to send out the chain letter you find the new issue of *Esquire Gentleman.*

A CALL TO THE COAST

1:05–1:32 p.m. *Esquire Gentleman.* Anyone for a bottle-green velvet dinner jacket?

1:33 p.m. Call Chip Ralston's scary publicist, Judith Viertel, in L.A. Secretary puts you on hold. And then over the receiver come the unmistakable strains in a Muzak version of Rod Stewart's "Do Ya Think I'm Sexy?" After you've listened to the whole song twice a voice breaks in—

"We're considering your request," she announces without preamble. You are astonished to be talking to her, Judith Viertel being the kind of publicist who practically has her own publicist—a fierce protector of the famous who is herself famously unavailable for bit players of the Fourth Estate like myself. "I'm faxing you a release specifying the parameters of acceptable questions and giving us approval of all quotations."

"I already signed, Judith. This was a done deal two weeks ago." Although you're not exactly proud of signing away your journalistic integrity, it's now standard operating procedure with the big stars, and it's not like we're talking about issues of national security here.

Judith herself invented this particular form of prior restraining order a couple of years ago.

"Chip's in discussions with Tarantino right now, and then he's got to edit his documentary on the election. I can't be bothering him with this kind of shit. I'll have somebody get back to you in the next week or two."

And then, without further ado, she's gone. And you, my friend, are screwed.

1:45 p.m. Shuffle to the newsstand for a pack of Seven Stars and the *Daily News*. You haven't really started smoking again, just a temporary thing till you get through this crisis. It comes back to you, though, no question. Inhale, exhale. Like riding a bike. From zero right back to a pack a day. Light one right here in front of the store. Suddenly worried you might be missing a phone call from Philomena, you hurry back, dodging deranged panhandlers and weaving back through the oldsters bundled up in their wheelchairs in front of the nursing home, mummifying in the winter sunlight.

AN INTERLUDE OF SELF-DISGUST

1:51 p.m. No messages.

2:00–2:13 p.m. All around you the city hums with purposive activity and commerce while you wallow in a slough of sloth and despond. Your life has no purpose and no direction. No wonder Philomena left. The phone rings, thankfully abbreviating this line of self-flagellation.

"I can't write," Jeremy says. "I can't even read. The *Times* review's been postponed." God bless him, another unproductive citizen of the metrop. You can hear Todd Rundgren's "It Wouldn't Have Made Any Difference" in the background.

"Maybe you'll get one of the guys."

"You want to have lunch?" he asks. "Isn't that what real people do, the civilians? Have lunch? Take lunch? *Do* lunch? What's the verb now? People with jobs and normal schedules. Correct me if I'm wrong, but don't they go to their offices and talk on the phone and go to meetings and save the world and then around about noon, twelve-thirty, they repair to coffee shops and restaurants to take on some well-earned calories, some charred mammal flesh on a bun or what have you, in the company of their *business associates*? I suppose," he continues, "that's one blessing about not having a real job. I don't ever have to use the phrase *business associates. Hello, this is Homer Lunchbox, my business associate. Shall we do lunch?*"

Many people might feel privileged to have Jeremy's schedule, to be the masters of their own time, but he often speaks as if he believes that his freedom and leisure are burdens inflicted on him by the lucky bastards who get to wake up to the alarm clock every morning and take a train to work, or for that matter to write mindless articles about empty-headed celebrities. This is what I love about Jeremy, his uncompromising unreasonableness.

I tell him I will be happy to try this crazy little thing called lunch, though truth be told I'm not very hungry.

AT THE EMPIRE DINER

"That tweedy asshole's staring at me."

"Why would he be staring at you?"

"I don't know, he probably hates Jews."

"Jeremy, you don't *look* like a Jew," I whisper. "Even your mother has her doubts. You look like a goddamn Swede. You look like Thor or Woden, for Christ's sake. Did you have a Scandinavian milkman when you were growing up?"

Whether or not the man in question, an aging prepster in Harris tweed, had any previous interest in Jeremy, he does turn toward us at this moment, revealing, it seems to me, a face that is more plausibly Semitic than my friend's.

"What's the matter?" Jeremy shouts. "You've never seen a Jew with long blond hair?" Holding up a hank of his blond mane.

An admirer of the sixties, Jeremy is still fighting the old battles, perhaps because he missed them at the time. Like the priest of a lost religion, he rails against the corruption of a society in which the Beatles' "Revolution" is used to sell sneakers.

"Is Lehmann-Haupt Jewish?" Jeremy asks.

"Actually," I say, "I have no idea."

"What's-her-fucking-name hates everybody except Anne fucking Tyler and Amy fucking Tan. I don't stand a chance. Wrong initials, wrong sex."

"When do I get a copy of the precious book?" I ask.

"You're on the list," he says. "Blaine's assistant's mailing the personal copies today."

We are sitting at the counter of this Platonic form of all diners, this chrome, black-and-white Art Deco photo stylist's wet dream of a beanery, waiting for our grilled cheese and tomato sandwiches. When we ordered a few minutes ago the counterman asked if we wanted them with bacon, and Jeremy erupted into a tirade about sulfites and nitrates, limited planetary resources and cruel and unusual methods of pig execution. I get nervous, therefore, when the man next to us orders a bacon cheeseburger. I am afraid that at the very least Jeremy will tell the man the story of his conversion: how, when he was eleven years old, he was driving with his parents and they passed a cattle truck on the highway, bearing a herd off to slaughter. Looking into the eyes of these cows, Jeremy had an epiphany, and pledged right then and there that he would never touch beef again. How Jeremy knew that these particular bovines were en route to the slaughterhouse I have never been able to determine. But he has stuck to his resolution for more than twenty years. Nothing with eyes.

While Jeremy would like to advise me about my problems, he has difficulty getting past his own. As a listener, he's like a man who can't ever quite seem to get out of the house; he keeps stopping at the door and turning back to get his scarf, checking to see if he accidentally left the stove on, and then suddenly the phone rings. . . .

Jeremy is too self-absorbed and tormented to spare much sympathy for others, but generally it is comforting to spend time with him because after getting an earful of Jeremy's inner life you feel blessed by comparison.

"When Natasha left me," he says, "I couldn't get out of bed for a month."

"You're *still* in bed, Jeremy."

"You're right," he says happily.

Natasha is the lost goddess of Jeremy's cult, the queen of a prelapsarian kingdom located in Middlebury, Vermont. They lived there together for six years, first as undergraduates and then as latter-day hippies, growing and eating vegetables, fucking and putting up fruit in Mason jars. As with Sean, the lamented Irish terrier, Jeremy didn't know what he had until it was gone, and he has been mourning it ever since. Although it has been seven years since Natasha left to find a room of her own, Jeremy speaks of their shared past, and the betrayal, as if it were yesterday. There have been other doomed romances, but Natasha is the primal wound, the pattern for all the others and for all his stories. In Jeremy's fiction, someone like Natasha is always leaving.

"Maybe she'll come back," I say.

"Natasha?"

"Philomena."

"She's gone, Connor. She's only coming back to get her clothes. Plus, watch, she'll take all the tapes and CDs you bought when you were together. They always do, even the ones they bitched about at the time. It doesn't matter that she absolutely hated *Led Zeppelin II* or *Louder Than Bombs*, it doesn't matter that she always told you to turn them down. She'll scoop 'em right up along with the complete works of the fucking Simon twins."

"You mean the Cocteau Twins."

"No, the Simon twins. Carly and Paul. Fucking *girl* music."

"For a vegetarian you're not very politically sound."

"Hey, do I look like a dork to you?"

Anyway, I think, I probably won't be able to listen to any of the old tunes, fraught as they will be with unbearable poignancy.

THE MAGIC OF TODD RUNDGREN, THE REGRETS OF CONNOR

Jeremy listens constantly to the Todd Rundgren albums which constituted the soundtrack of his long idyll with Natasha. The ones he bought to replace the ones she took with her. As he reiterates between bites of his sandwich, he considers Todd the underheralded genius of recent times. Meanwhile, I am thinking about the ways in which I failed to keep Philomena happy:

- Withholding affection, perverse little gestures in the domestic struggle for dominance.
- Not kissing her as much as she wanted or perhaps needed to be kissed, gratuitous kissing somehow falling out of your repertoire after a year or so of living together.
- All the mornings you got annoyed when she tried to share something from the newspaper, acting put out about having your own reading interrupted.
- The Danish woman you made out with at Temple Bar.
- All the flowers you failed to bring home after the first few months.
- Pallas.
- Your unforgivable snobbery, most especially on the evening she tried to share her delight and wonder after reading Raymond Carver for the first time. "He's really great," she said, and you said, "Hey, tell me something I didn't know."
- Being proud of the fact that she was a model.
- That actress in L.A.

No wonder she ran off with some other guy. What took her so long?

THE WISDOM OF PAI-CHING

"You haven't touched your sandwich," Jeremy points out, eyeing it with interest. Whatever his claims to sloth, he has already jogged five miles today, his standard practice, which presumably works up the appetite; I wouldn't know.

"Yeah, well." Charred and shiny with grease on my plate, it looks vaguely hostile. "The great Zen roshi Pai-Ching tells us, 'If one does not work for a day, one should not eat for a day.' "

"Zen, Schmen," says Jeremy. "The Chinese and the fucking Japanese, they're not real Buddhists. Any society that systematically indulges in wholesale whale killing, live monkey-brain eating, and the bloodthirsty harvest of endangered species for their alleged aphrodisiac body parts cannot call itself Buddhist. Plus Zen was what ruined Salinger. I mean, once he got into that one-hand-clapping shit it was all over."

"You want the sandwich or not?"

Jeremy switches plates while I stare balefully at a young couple smooching in a booth.

"Maybe I should just get in my car and drive," he muses. "Leave the state before the paper comes out, go someplace where they don't get the *Times*, where they hate New York."

CHAIN LETTER, CONT.

This letter has been around the world in a hundred and eighty days. Connor McKnight left the letter sitting on his desk. A week after receiving it his girlfriend packed up her diaphragm and disappeared. Two weeks later Connor discovered the letter on his desk. He sent out twenty copies and subsequently his girlfriend returned and said she loved him. It seems she had been hit by a taxicab in a foreign city and suffered a case of amnesia. The day after her boyfriend mailed this letter she regained her memory and came home. The day after her return, Connor found a paper bag on the street containing $2,830,520 in cash. They were married a week later and now divide their time between St. Bart's, Aspen and Tamarindo.

MISCEGENATION SPECULATION

Here's something I've been awaiting for about the last ten years: the first high-profile marriage of a Hollywood sex goddess to a Japanese billionaire. The fact that this hasn't happened already is inexplicable without reference to Japanese xenophobia. With a little help from good old American racism. These kinds of insights—and I have them all the time—could be worth money. Thinking that this particular area of inquiry nicely combined my underutilized background in Japanese studies with my beat as celebrity chronicler, I once tried to interest Jillian Crowe in an essay on this subject. Glasses on top of her head, Jackie style, she asked, "Connor, darling, do I honestly look like the editor of the *New York Review of Books* to you?"

OUR HEROINE CHECKS IN

Just leaving the apartment when I hear Philomena's voice on the machine: "Hi. You there? Guess not." Sounding none too eager to find otherwise, all too ready to hang up without a struggle.

As rapidly as any actor in Stetson ever unholstered a Colt Peacemaker I snatch the receiver from its cradle. "Where the hell are you?"

The silence lasts long enough for me to fear I've scared her off, like the fisherman who yanks his rod at the first flutter of the bobber. Finally, the line tightens from the other end: "That doesn't really matter."

"Come home. Please. No questions asked."

"I think I need some time to think."

"Phil, what are you doing? Where are you?" God, my voice sounds pathetic, tremulous, quavering between tenor and falsetto.

"Things haven't exactly been so great with us lately."

"I'll be better. I'll be so good you'll think I'm someone else."

"You're not so bad, Connor."

"Then why aren't you here?"

"Look, I've got to go."

"Who are you with?" I demand, desperately changing modes.

"I'm . . . not with anybody." I don't need a polygraph to confirm that the rhythm and tone of this response are all wrong.

"So why did you take your diaphragm?" I ask. "Who are you fucking while you're taking all this contemplative Virginia Woolf *Room of One's Own* time to think?"

A benighted sigh. "Goodbye, Connor."

"My parents are coming to town," I say, lamely. I believe this is called—in the terminology of logic—appeal to false authority.

"Say hi for me."

"That'll warm their hearts."

"I'll call in a few days," she says. And she's gone.

Deranged by jealousy and grief, I feel even worse—if such a thing is possible—when I realize I have forgotten to warn her about the letter, that she might be in danger. Furious at her for not allowing me to protect her.

E-MAIL

To: Scribbler@aol.com
From: Jenrod@inch.com
Subject: Chaos
Did you like the picture? I'll be at Chaos day after tomorrow.
Midnight. See U there? I'll recognize you for sure.

To: Jenrod@inch.com
From: Scribbler@aol.com
Subject: Your Kind Invitation
My parents are coming to town, always an ordeal, and I doubt
that I will feel much like dancing. However, if I haven't hung
myself from the shower rod by then—who knows? But you had
better start without me.

INVENTORY

Between drinks I sift through Philomena's possessions, the vodka bottle within reach. First her modeling portfolio, the many beautiful moods of Philomena: funky in Sui; sultry in lingerie; laughing amidst a clatch of gorgeous Merit smokers; but more often blank, pouty, staring beyond the lens. The New Model Demeanor, an expression beyond expression — the look that says, *Not only will you never look like this, not only will you never touch this, but I'm not even going to work for you.* The exquisite boredom of the mannequin. *Let the actors act, let them pretend to be something, I'm young and beautiful and I desire nothing.* In these pix Phil looks so frighteningly like all the other models — the way the saints in Byzantine mosaics all look the same — that I can't always be sure it *is* Phil.

Dozens of pages of contact sheets. In her desk: a packet of birthday and Valentine cards from yours truly, tied in a pink ribbon, which I set aside, not presently feeling strong enough to read them. The other cards and letters are revealing only by virtue of their scarcity: a single letter from a model she roomed with in Tokyo; infrequent postcards from her mother, chillingly newsy; a brief monogrammed note from my own mother congratulating her on her appearance in a Gap ad. A file folder with all of my published articles. Assorted amusing items from the *New York Post*, and a page from last month's *Vogue* on Chip Ralston with *FYI* scrawled over the headline — the gesture of a helpmeet. She was always saving items for me in her restless grazing of the glossies. Surely at the moment she so thoughtfully clipped this she wasn't thinking of leaving me. Finally, a draft of my lost and unlamented screenplay, *The Simple Life,* an offbeat romantic comedy about a writer and a model, inscribed on the cover page: *To Phil, my muse, leading lady of my heart.*

No secret journal. No trace of him — my enemy. Looking at the mirror she broke the night before she left, I wonder: How many years bad luck?

The clothes in her dresser are erotically mnemonic: here the skirt I pulled down in a frenzy one afternoon, here the sweater I was too impatient to remove on the same occasion. The generous, empty cups of her bras a painful synecdoche for her absence.

PSYCHOPHARMACOLOGY

"Maybe she's telling the truth," I say. "Maybe she just needs time." After a sleepless night, I am in Brooke's apartment, watching her smoke a joint.

"You'd better have some of this," she says.

"You know I don't like drugs that make me feel stupid. I feel stupid enough to begin with. I like the drugs that make me feel incredibly smart, only I can't afford them."

"I *want* to feel stupid," says Brooke.

"You have more IQ to spare than the rest of us."

"Have you heard that song: *Don't want to get stoned, / But I don't want to not get stoned?*"

"When did you start keeping up with popular culture?"

"Some band called . . . the Melonheads? Is that right? Did that guy die of an OD? I don't know." She examines the tarred, smoking roach as if it might tell her—I'm not about to, since she'll make fun of me for knowing. Finally she asks, "Have you tried any of these new smart drugs I hear about?"

"If you ever watched the boys and girls at a rave, you wouldn't hold out a lot of hope for the brain boost of putative smart drugs. I've always found, however, that if you add a couple shots of vodka, at least you *feel* smart."

"Connor, in your view, is there anything to which one doesn't add vodka?"

"Give me a sec. I'm thinking."

"Don't hurt yourself."

"Bourbon."

"What about it?"

"Something to which one doesn't add vodka."

"Jesus. You sure you don't want some of this? Little hit?"

"Only if you can guarantee it will bring Phil back."

"It's just an herb, not an industrial-strength toxin." She giggles. "What was the name of that band you liked?" she asks. "Retarded Youth?"

"Sonic Youth? Arrested Development?"

"Sounds like you either way."

The good thing about Brooke's smoking pot: maybe she'll get the munchies.

"Don't tell Mom and Dad about Philomena," I warn her as we head out to meet them.

TEA EN FAMILLE

"Geronimo," Brooke says when we bail out of the cab in front of the St. Regis.

And there they are—Mom and Dad, having a little chat with the waiter in the King Cole Bar. We sneak up and greet them awkwardly. Does everyone feel shy when they first see their parents again, or is it just me? The feeling being: Yes, of course I remember you, but I hope to God you've forgotten that thing I did with the cantaloupe when I was fourteen. My mother hugs me unreservedly, smelling faintly of sunshine and oil paint. My father and I have a special dodge-and-feint routine which results in a kind of brief, manly half-embrace. Unless he's drunk. So the good news is he's sober, or else he'd be clinging to my neck and telling me that he just wants me to know that he loves me in spite of everything and he really hopes—and he's not just saying this—that he hasn't been too really *awful* a father.

"Brooke, darling," says Mom. "Have you been sick?"

"Good God, Brooke," blurts Dad. "You look like you've been at Auschwitz."

"I do wish," Brooke says, "people would stop frivolously invoking one of the major horrors of the century for purposes of cheap physical analogies."

"She's had the flu," I say, instinctively covering for her.

"I thought," says Dad, "we'd gotten over this problem after Madeira."

"There's been a lot of flu this year," Mom says helpfully. "I think it comes from Hong Kong, like so many other things. Your father and I went there four or five years ago and it was really absolutely fascinating. All these Chinese people. Dad got me the most beautiful string of . . ." She drifts off for a moment, as is her wont, her attention snagged by something in the middle distance.

"String of teeth?" says Brooke.

"What a perfectly wonderful idea—a string of teeth," Mom says. "I used to save your baby teeth. I wonder what happened to them?" She seems stumped. "Let's have a drink, shall we? A festive cocktail?"

The waiter has rematerialized at this opportune moment.

"Tea for me," says red-eyed, righteous Brooke.

Mom starts humming "Tea for Two," pausing to order her own drink. "Do you think I might just have some Campari with a little bit of sweet vermouth and a splash of seltzer." The waiter raises his pencil from the pad with a flourish, as if to say it is his pleasure to entertain strange drink orders, but Mom isn't quite finished. "With a slice of orange . . . in a snifter." She shapes a big bowl with her hands. "And do you think could you float a little teensy bit of gin on top?"

The waiter is reeling.

"Basically," I explain, "my mom wants a negroni on the rocks with a splash of soda."

Brooke says, "I'm sure that clears things right up, Connor."

"Is *that* what I ordered?" Mom asks, smiling at me, her very bright child. "It sounds so sophisticated the way you say it."

Dad can hardly contain his impatience and barks his order: a Johnnie Walker Black with soda. Good manly stuff. He drinks Red at home, Black on special occasions. In his book, both are equally efficacious. With a cringe of apology directed toward Brooke, I order a Bloody Mary. Yes, I find it cheers up the tomato juice considerably, that little splash of vodka. These fucking potheads can get very self-righteous about alcohol, though it's true that no one in my family ought to be encouraged to drink. Not that Mom and Dad have ever needed any encouragement. Just point them at the bar and stand back.

"The city looks very festive," Mom says.

"We tried to fluff it up for your arrival," Brooke says. "Connor put up a humongous evergreen over in Rockefeller Center and I tied a giant red bow around Cartier."

"My clever ones."

"So, what do you think of your mayor?" Dad asks me. I almost get the impression that he imagines that I sit down every so often with Rudy and discuss the future of the metropolis over drinks.

"Actually," I say, "he kind of gives me the willies."

My father frowns. "Well, I'll tell you one thing. You could sure as hell use a Republican mayor in this crazy town."

Speech suddenly seems perilous with so many subjects to be avoided—Brooke's anorexia, Dad's drinking, politics.

"Let me give you just one example," he says. "Waldorf-Astoria. New York landmark, right? Classmate of mine, Billy Buxton, Billy was general manager when they renovated the place, must've been fifteen, twenty years ago. Endless delays, holdups, thefts of material. Just for instance, one day the carpenter's union gets mad at the plumber's union. So what do you think they do? Pour cement in all the drains in every last room. Little prank to register their unhappiness with the plumbers. Every single pipe in the building has to be ripped out to the tune of a few million smackeroos. Did the carpenters pay for that? I don't think so. The plumbers picked up double overtime to pull the pipes out and replace them. After the carpenters had ripped open the walls for them. That . . . ," he says, pointing a finger at my sternum, "that's a New York Story for you."

"Naked city," says Brooke.

"You look tired, Connor," says Mom. "Have you been just working yourself to death up here?" It is Mom's opinion that Yankees, and especially New Yorkers, work far too hard and long, thereby compromising their health and serenity. If she only knew.

"Connor's been making the world safe for celebrity," says my adoring sister.

"I just don't know how you-all do it," says Mom, her tone combining admiration and exhaustion.

"Some of us don't," Brooke replies.

"It's no wonder," Mom says, "you had to take a rest from that dreadful school of yours."

"What, exactly," Dad ventures, "is your status at the university?"

"I'm on basket-weaving leave," says Brooke.

"I mean to say . . ." But whatever Dad means to say is thankfully lost as the waiter arrives, as welcome as the mail boat pulling into a South Sea harbor.

"Cocktails," Mom announces brightly as she hoists the skewered orange slice from her drink and inspects it. "California," she concludes.

Dad signals for the waiter, who scurries over. "My wife would like a slice of plump, juicy Florida orange in her cocktail."

"Beg your pardon?"

"As opposed to this desiccated wedge of California . . . whatever. Could you forward that request up the chain of command?"

The waiter says he'll see what he can do.

"Bing Crosby," says Dad. "Remember that little piece of business? He takes our money, does the ads for Florida. Then turns around and puts his money into Sunkist. Makes a fortune on those dried-out California navels. It's an arid state, for Christ's sake. A desert. How the hell do they expect to grow a juicy delicious citrus product?"

Mom informs us that a near neighbor's orchard in Florida has . . .

THE SPREADING DECLINE

which comes from a worm—called a nematode—that feeds on the roots of orange trees (which in Florida are invariably grafted on the rootstock of lemon trees, but that's another story). The tree dies slowly, from the top down, while the yield steadily decreases. The spreading decline was frequently invoked by the male parent as the ultimate and inevitable judgment on those children who didn't appreciate just how lucky they were to have a large, watertight roof over their heads.

THE SILK ROUTE

Later, after the hospitality director has promised my father to inquire into the possibility of using Florida oranges for all the hotel's juice and garnish needs, we take a family stroll up Fifth Avenue, gazing glazily at the little gemlike Tiffany windows with their gingerbread Christmasy landscapes, then slice briskly through the bright crunchy air of late November over to Hermès to buy Dad his annual Christmas tie. With a pang I recall that last year I bought Philomena (among many other excellent presents I couldn't afford) a horsey, colorful Hermès scarf. As I recall she liked it, liked the vision it conjured of some future self as a respectable Park Avenue lady swinging her perfect shoulder-length coif across Seventy-fifth Street on her way to lunch at Mortimer's. Certainly she liked it better than the Marc Brouwer dress, with its formfitting clinginess and plunging neckline. "What are you trying to do, pimp me?" she demanded. No, God no, not that, though it occurs to me I might have been guilty of trying to show her off just a bit. But I didn't want other guys to *fuck* her, *honest*. I just wanted other guys to *want* to fuck her. There's a big difference.

Disposed as I am at this moment to blame myself, I am also aware that it could easily have gone the other way last Christmas, depending on the sheerest of whims: Philomena might have been furious at the scarf, taken it as a sign that I saw her as aging and frumpy. . . .

Not that I'm complaining. Really, I'm not. Come home. All's forgiven.

"What do you mean there's no Christmas tie this time of year," Dad demands of the clerk. "There's *always* a Christmas tie."

"I'm afraid we didn't do an actual Christmas tie per se this year, sir."

"But I always buy the Christmas tie," my father says unhappily. "Every year." At this moment it is easy to imagine him as a small boy. Like me when I wanted the minibike for Christmas and got the deluxe chemistry set instead.

Mom and Dad go on to Brooks Brothers, the next stop on the McKnight New York circuit. Advent Stations of the Cross. Dad is irritated when I excuse myself. It's a family thing, going to Brooks, getting the big nod from the old-fart salesmen who have been waiting on Dad for years. I plead work at the office, agreeing to meet them later at Wally's and Joseph's.

"Oh, let's do see your office," suggests Mom. "Isn't it right near Brooks Brothers?"

"There's really nothing to see," I say truthfully. Although if she met my parents, Jillian might be inclined to cut me some slack. "Really, go on and enjoy the town. I'll catch you at seven."

DEUS EX MACHINA

Back at the apartment, I find a box from the phone company in the entry hall. Inside is my brand-new phone unit with digital-display window featuring caller ID. I connect the phone as per instructions and stare at it hopefully, but I'm no more successful in willing Philomena to call than I am at telepathically commanding Brooke to eat.

THANKSGIVING CHEER

Recently in the *New York Times* Frank Prial wrestled with that perennial question: what wine to match with your Thanksgiving turkey and traditional fixings. Some say champagne, some chardonnay. Frank leans toward zinfandel, and there's even a case to be made for a young cabernet sauvignon. Be advised that my father recommends Johnnie Walker Black, over ice, mixed with moderate amounts of club soda or seltzer water. Cuts right through the tart sweetness of the cranberry sauce which makes Thanksgiving wine matching so tricky. And none of these pretentious single malts, thank you very much. Thanksgiving dinner at the St. Regis. Traditionalists that we are, Mom and I are working on a bottle of champagne. Mom has pronounced the bubbles "very festive."

Doug, old Mad Dog himself, is throwing back the Diet Cokes like there's no tomorrow. Brooke is sipping mint tea, like the hippie she once was, glaring at the food, or at least I think she is, though she has yet to remove her sunglasses, a detail which would hardly bear mentioning in the more fashionable precincts of New York, but Brooke is scrupulously untrendy. What I find most curious is that no one has decided to comment on Brooke's shades, not even my father, whose notions of pukka comportment and sartorial propriety are so severe.

"I love Thanksgiving," Mom says.

"I find it difficult to give thanks," Brooke mutters, "when so many people in the world are suffering tonight."

"Give thanks you're not one of them," says Dad, tucking into a fresh scotch.

"In Mogadishu a family of four doesn't see this much protein in a month."

"You must see a lot of suffering," Mom says to Doug. I still don't understand why he had to come. Doesn't he have his own fucked-up family to annoy?

Doug shrugs stoically, making himself appear for a moment even more neckless than usual.

TRAUMA, THEORY AND PRACTICE

"Is there a special season," Mom asks, "or a time of the month or anything when you get more traumas than other times?"

Dad snuffles at this question—that nasal exclamation of a man who is at once accustomed to, and yet never ceases to be amazed by, the eccentricity of his wife's questions.

"No, actually, that's a good question," Doug says, answering Dad's snort. "The full moon is the worst. Emergency rooms are always extremely frenetic the night of a full moon. We see more knife and gunshot wounds. I don't really know how to explain it scientifically, but the empirical evidence is fairly convincing. What's easier to account for is the fact that sick children, particularly from economically disadvantaged neighborhoods, tend to be brought to the emergency room after eleven p.m."

Mom looks happily perplexed. "And why is that?"

"Because that's when prime-time television ends."

"The children wait until after prime time to get sick?"

"I believe," Dad says, "Brooke's, uh, *friend* means that the *parents* wait until after their favorite shows are over before they bother to bring the little urchins in."

"That's dreadful." Mom turns to Doug. "Is that true?"

Doug nods sadly.

"I assume," Dad says, "we're speaking of the economically disadvantaged."

"The worst are the self-mutilators," says Brooke, rising out of her stupor to do a brief promotional spot for her beau. "Can you imagine having a ward full of desperately ill and injured people to tend to, and having to spend two hours on some guy who, well, tell them about that thing yesterday. . . ."

"Well," says Doug, "I wish I could say it was a unique case, but in fact we've seen it before. Patient arrived on the ward yesterday under his own power, clutching a towel to his groin, we estimate he lost more than thirty percent of his blood."

"Don't tell me," says Dad.

"Fortunately, his sister had recovered the, uh, penis, and put it on ice."

"He cut it off himself?" asks Mom.

"I'd think," I say, "you'd bleed to death."

"No actually, curiously enough, in a clean, perpendicular cut the veins tend to dilate and self-seal, as it were—"

"Doug spent ten hours in surgery," says Brooke.

"Now, on the other hand, if the penis were sliced diagonally, there would be a much greater danger of fatal blood loss since the veins—"

"Stop, for God's sake!" Dad shouts. "Is this any kind of dinner table conversation."

I don't know, I kind of agree with the old man, although I can't help feeling a healthy sort of morbid curiosity, not to mention a twinge of sympathy for Doug, the outsider, who draws his head down even farther into his shoulders like a scared turtle. I mean, it's a little unseemly, this skilled healer cowed by my elegantly useless father.

Brooke says, "God forbid a little reality with our happy repast."

"Doug," says Mom, "are you sure you wouldn't like a *teeny* bit of champagne? Or a nice cocktail? Something with a bit of fruit and fizz?"

MORE BEVERAGE NOTES

One factor Frank Prial doesn't take into account about holiday potables is their combustibility. When long-separated members of the same family are soaked in spirits and rubbed together, explosions almost inevitably result. Maybe the turkey is a catalyst of some sort. This year it happens after I ask Mom how she met Dad. It's a story I haven't heard in years, certainly never with the vivid dramatic detail she gives it this afternoon.

BOY MEETS GIRL, SPRING 1955

"We used to think Williams boys were so square," she says, sipping delicately at her champagne, the stem of the flute pinched lightly between age-spotted pointer and thumb. "And of course they were."

A curmudgeonly harrumph from my father here, who could almost pass for a square college boy, still dressed in the uniform of his preppy youth—blue blazer, blue oxford button-down shirt and regimental tie—his pink, pickled face unlined by the tussles of commerce or metaphysics.

"We used to think Bennington girls were artsy-fartsy dykes," counters my father, who, after all, was the captain of the debating team.

"And the Williams boys were so very tolerant of diversity," Mom continues, winking at us. "But we had to admit they were awfully good-looking." She smiles sweetly at my father, who pretends not to be interested in this story. Beneath her sun-and-nicotine cured skin, Mom's still girlish, her pale blue eyes childishly bright, her long hair worn just as it was at Bennington, the gold now ghosted with silver.

"I drove down with Cassie Reymond and some other girls. Cassie was an actress who later moved to New York and last I heard she was married to that actor who was in that wonderful play, what was it called, about the—it wasn't with Richard Burton but somebody like that?" She looks hopefully at my father, who coughs impatiently into his hand.

"*Camelot?*" Doug proposes.

Oh, *do* shut up, Doug.

Beside us, a silent Japanese family, oblivious to the feast of the Pilgrims, wraps itself around some steaks. Father, mother, two solemn preteen daughters in severe white blouses and pageboy haircuts.

"Anyway, we got there and it was awful, all these fierce, shy, hungry boys in their nice J. Press suits and their crewcuts, waiting to pounce. We drove down in Cassie's car, thank God, but there was a bus that arrived from Smith or somewhere like that, someplace frilly and proper, maybe Holyoke I don't know. Anyway, this bus came just as we pulled in and the boys were just waiting there. They formed a kind of gauntlet or gamut—what is it? I can never get those two things straight. Is gauntlet the glove that you throw down when you challenge somebody to a duel, or is that gamut? Anyway this was the other one."

"*Gauntlet* is actually the word you're looking for," says Doug. "I think," he hedges, for modesty's sake.

"And then there's *gimlet*," says Mom. Speaking of words.

Here at the St. Regis they serve the fancy, lumpy cranberry

sauce with real berries, but I prefer the cheap jellied kind. It
appears that I am the only one paying any attention at all to his
food. No, actually—Brooke seems to be carving a mandala in her
mashed potatoes. "So," she says, looking up wearily. "As far as I can
tell nothing happened. Maybe you and Dad never actually met.
Which would account for this feeling I have that I'm not *really*
here. Which would account for this continuing ontological skepticism with regard to myself."

"Oh, we met, all right," Mom assures her. "I spotted your father
hovering halfway through the dance. He was dressed exactly the
way he is now—blue blazer and a blue oxford-cloth button-down
shirt and the striped tie. Could be the same tie." My father looks
down at the neckwear in question, pennant of some lost regiment
of the king's army, and shakes his head. In fact he went to Brooks
Brothers yesterday in order to stock up on these very items, these
crucial components of the uniform which tell my father and the
world who he is. "He was kind of cute square," Mom continues.
"And, oh, I remember—he was wearing saddle shoes."

"Not I," my father says, but I could see he was enjoying this.
"White bucks, maybe."

"You were. That was almost the cutest part about you, your nervous little brown-and-white feet."

"My feet are *not* little. Nine and a half C." He turns to Doug.
"You call that little?"

"He kept making these circles around us, getting a tiny bit
closer with each swing, all nonchalant and pretending not to
notice me, though of course it was hard to tell which girl he was
pretending not to notice, since there were four of us and he was so
pointedly oblivious. Well, he panicked when they announced the
last song—I think it was 'Smoke Gets in Your Eyes.' "

My mother breaks off her narrative to warble a bar: "*They asked
me how I knew / My true love was true . . .*"

"What's the matter with you?" my father demands, noting my
suddenly crumpled demeanor. Philomena and I used to love that
song in its Bryan Ferry version. And now here I am, acting it out.

"And when another boy asked me to dance," Mom resumes, "I

realized it was me he'd been pretending not to notice because his face just collapsed, he just wilted as this flattop boy with no neck trotted me off. I could feel those lovely sad blue eyes watching as we danced."

My father snorts in disapproval of this pitiful portrait. "Oh, come now."

"Well, I dragged my feet on the way out—if I'd walked any slower I think I would've taken root in the pavement like a big old cypress tree in a swamp—and I was just about to give up on him when I felt a hand on my shoulder in the parking lot."

"What'd he say," asks Brooke.

"He asked me if I wanted a tour of the campus."

Brooke hoots with laughter. "At least he didn't ask you to see his etchings."

Dad turns pink as a boiled shrimp. The Japanese family aims their solemn dark eyes at us, strange noisy gaijin. *Ah, so desu—this is typical American family.*

"I did *not* say that," Dad insists.

H O W   T O   G E T   Y O U R   B E A U
T O   P O P   T H E   Q U E S T I O N

"Well, I didn't really need to see the campus, but I told him I'd love to go someplace where we could talk. So we ended up sitting in his roommate's Buick. And of course the talking led to kissing. I thought he was just a wonderful kisser, and after about ten minutes I realized he was just in agony, and so of course I wanted to help him. It seemed like the least I could do."

"Lillie!"

"And the poor sweet boy was so grateful he proposed to me right there in the back of the Buick."

"What," Brooke asks, "you gave him a blow job?"

"Young lady!"

"Heavens, no," says Mom, "I just, you know, used my hand."

DAD DEMURS

"This is not family conversation!" Dad thumps the table with his fist, making shimmery waves on our beverages.

"You got a proposal out of a hand job?" Brooke's impressed, Doug nonplussed. Meanwhile, I'm thinking back on my luncheon encounter with Pallas; perhaps I should've proposed, offered to take her away from all this. . . . But where? And once upon a time, when we were still mad for each other and conscious of it every moment, Philomena gave me a hand job in a cab. Why didn't I propose to her then? Why didn't I ever? God, I was stupid. If only I had, she'd be sitting here now, eating Thanksgiving dinner, comparing notes on postejaculatory proposals with my mom. *Well, when I jerked Connor off in that cab, right before the cabbie told us to get out, he just up and asked me on the spot.* What she'd be seeing at this exact moment, if she were here, is my father rising unsteadily to his feet like a booster rocket on the launchpad, wobbling, shrugging off the clench of gravity. He nearly tips over as he unexpectedly reaches full extension, but quickly regains the vertical. "This is not . . . I simply won't have it."

He slams his open hand on the table to get our attention, snaring that of our fellow diners as well.

The Japanese are agog. Is this a typical American custom?

The waiter dashes over. "Is everything all right, Mr. McKnight?"

"Oh, everything is just grand. Just marvelous. My wife wants the whole world to know about our intimate relations. A nice family discussion about hand jobs on Thanksgiving Day." No question, he has the attention of the entire room now. The captain is edging over our way, and the other diners have turned away from their turkey and stuffing and their own pallid conversations. Dad notes this, and seems to start playing to the room. I recognize the look in his eye. He had the same look just before he launched the turkey across the dining room a couple years back.

"Splendid. Hand jobs in the old Buick. Maybe over Christmas

dinner we can talk about oral sex. My daughter seems to favor that subject. Lovely. Why don't we just let it all hang out, as you kids say. Very modern. Silly of me to cling to these old-fashioned notions of decency and modesty. Behind the times. Nothing's taboo, nothing's sacred. It's on television every day now, people falling all over themselves to reveal their most intimate filthy secrets. Splendid. Tell America, tell your own son and daughter all about their father's sex life. Brooke, Connor, anything else you'd like to know? Anything your mom's left out? Maybe she'd like to tell you about my private . . . parts. We could go on TV. That would be very modern. Excellent. Why don't we just have a show-and-tell."

The captain has arrived just behind and to the right of my father's chair; he intervenes quickly, but not quickly enough, as Dad unzips his fly.

The two young Japanese girls at the next table simultaneously raise their hands to cover their mouths, though not their eyes. Their mother squeals—I can't help wondering if she's thinking about comparative anatomy—and then it seems to me the room falls silent.

Even *I* am stunned, accustomed though I am to our dramatic family gestures. When my father throws his arms open in a gesture of theatrical finale, the captain instinctively reaches down toward the exposed member, then snaps his hand back, just short of its apparent goal, as if he'd been bitten, judgment triumphing at the last moment over impulse. The problem, from his point of view, seems insuperable: how to conceal the offending organ without touching it. My father seems to grasp his dilemma, and to delight in it. His anger has metamorphosed, through the miraculous alchemy of alcohol, into perverse glee. The lawgiving patriarch has switched places with the anarchic child. Grinning impishly, he plants his hands on his hips in defiance of the would-be guardians of propriety.

The waiter, on a sudden inspiration, removes the serviette from his forearm and gingerly tucks it into the waist of Dad's gray flannels. And finally, after several eternities, the captain and the waiter together succeed in leading him off. "Just trying to catch up with the times," he tells them. "Trying to satisfy the curiosity of my loved ones. My beloved family, such a goddamn comfort to me in my declining years. . . ."

I sit grimacing at Brooke—who looks back at me with a kind of jaded chagrin—and try to pretend that I am not in this room, that my father did not just whip out his dick in Lespinasse in front of forty or fifty people, that they are not still staring at us, the family from hell, that Mad Dog was not here to witness this mortification so that on top of everything else I have to suffer a sense of familial embarrassment vis-à-vis Doug.

Here's what I'm thinking: If I had the choice of turning back the clock five minutes so that this never happened, or living through it all again and having Philomena back, faithful and happy, which would I choose?

"I thought it was a cute story," says Mom.

Of course I would choose Phil.

"It was, Mom." Brooke pats her papery, sun-speckled wrist. "I think we all really enjoyed it, except possibly Dad. Connor, you'd better go find him."

"No, actually I think I'll just rush down to City Hall and change my name, thanks."

"I'll go," says Doug, the helpful bastard.

"All right," I say. "I'm going, I'm going."

"He's never done that before," Mom notes for the record.

MORE WINE NOTES

Attn: Frank Prial: I am thinking, for next year's apéritif, maybe a nice glass of hemlock.

STILL OUT THERE, SOMEWHERE

Returning to the apartment, I flop down on the sofa, looking forward to some analgesic football. To someone from another country, this gnashing of bodies would appear chaotic, and yet there is a deep pattern here, helpfully illustrated by the commentators after each play. Even if there's no analogy with my own lurching progress, it's nice to watch some other guys get beat up for a change. And yet the choking melancholy seems only to mount within me. Finally I realize that the nubbly wool of the sofa is redolent of Philomena—the sweet smell of her soaps and unguents as well as the deeper, funkier scents—that my head is placed exactly where she usually sits, and I recall that the last time I saw her sitting in this spot she was gamely reading Faulkner's *Wild Palms*, looking up from her gorgeous trance to ask me vocabulary questions . . . and once again my eyes cloud over with tears. After at least a dozen tear-free years I have become a veritable artesian well.

Nose to the cushion, I am furiously attempting to masturbate when Philomena's phone chirps in the bedroom. Member in hand—his father's son—I walk over to the door to listen for the message, hoping for a clue, hearing only a series of clicks and beeps, the hiss of the answering tape. I'm already back on the couch when I realize that it's *her*—checking her messages from wherever she may be.

Racing back to the bedroom, tearing the receiver from its cradle. "Phil, hello, is that you? Please, don't hang up. Talk to me, will you? For Christ's sake. Where are you?"

"Hello, Connor," she says gravely, after a long silence. As though she knew of a terminal illness about which the doctors have not yet informed me, the patient. "I thought you'd be out with your family."

"I was."

"How are they?"

"Please. One sordid melodrama at a time. Phil, come home."

No response to this plea.

"Where *are* you?"

"I'm . . . it doesn't make any difference."

"Or should I say, with who?"

"Don't you mean *whom*?"

"What is this—levity?" I scream. "You wouldn't even know the difference if I hadn't taught you."

Another silence at the other end. I'm horrified at my own lack of charity, not only because I fear she'll hang up.

"I'm sorry, Phil, I didn't mean . . . I'm just sick with missing you and thinking about you fucking some—"

"Connor, don't. This is about you and me. It doesn't have anything to do with anybody else."

"Then why do I think it's about you trading up in the world?"

"Maybe you have low self-esteem."

"No shit."

Just when I can't think of what else to say I remember the threatening letter. I tell her about it, offer to go get it, though I'm glad when she tells me not to bother, since she'd probably hang up in the interval.

"It's this guy who saw me in GQ. He's mad because I didn't respond to his marriage proposal."

"What, you have a relationship with this fucking guy?"

"No. He's just written me some fan letters."

"How come I never heard about this?"

"I don't know."

"I guess there's a lot you haven't been telling me."

The silence stretches out. At least she's still on the other end, and we're not actually fighting. I'm loath to intrude on this hushed respite, and after a minute or more I begin to cherish it as a kind of intimacy. As an observer, I become curious about how long it will last, until I become fearful that she may break off before I've had a chance to state my case, whatever that might be.

"Do I know him?" I ask at last.

"The letter guy?"

"No, the diaphragm guy."

She sighs. "Maybe we should just focus on practical things," she says. "Can we do that, please? I'm sending a moving company over next week. Do you think you could be there to let them in?"

"Do you still love me *at all*?"

"Don't ask me that."

"Did you ever?"

"Don't be ridiculous, Connor."

The sound of my name on her lips is exquisite torture. "That's my role. To be ridiculous. That's the part I get to play in this little farce aspiring to tragedy."

"You're not ridiculous. Except when you talk like that." She laughs. "Who else would say 'this little farce aspiring to tragedy.' "

"Come home." My voice a pathetic birdlike squawk, its tonality undeniably ridiculous.

"Don't make this harder than it has to be."

"I don't quite see how it's been so terrifically backbreakingly hard on you. You haven't even . . . you haven't been willing to face me or even talk to me. Seems to me like you've made it pretty goddamn easy on yourself so far."

"You had three years to talk to me, Connor. You *don't* talk. At least not to me."

"I talk."

"Not about your feelings."

Could this be true? I don't think so. Well, maybe. I don't know, I thought there would be plenty of time for that later; I thought it was bad manners to yammer away about your problems. "I could learn," I say. "Okay? I could, you know, learn how."

"It's too late, Connor."

"Why is it too late? Don't say that." Tears are sluicing down my cheeks, leaking into the holes in the mouthpiece of the Princess-model phone. It might be simplest if I were suddenly electrocuted here, crying into Philomena's telephone. Except that I have one last desperate gesture to make: "Phil, I want you to marry me."

A year ago, six or even three lousy months ago, Philomena would have crawled through the phone to say yes. Not that I flatter myself with the idea that being yoked to me forever is so irresistible. But I do believe the idea of marriage seemed to her the perfect cure for a complex of yearnings and disappointments, most notably an imperfect childhood; and I was the logical candidate if only because I was *there*. We talked about it, alluded to its eventuality in that sensible way of couples who have lived together a long time. And indeed, she was waiting. She hinted, no, she actually stated outright that she wouldn't wait forever. That there were other men who thought she was pretty great, who would leap at the chance. Warning me about this very moment, when it would be too late because she would be gone. Yes, I remember now. But what the fuck was I thinking about then? I don't know what I was doing. Waiting for absolute certainty, I guess. I should've listened to Brooke when she was trying to explain Heisenberg and Gödel; apparently they don't even have that kind of certitude in math and science anymore.

"We'll move out of New York, get a little house somewhere. Live the simple life."

Now it's Philomena's turn to cry when she finally sobs, in response to my outrageously belated offer: "Connor, don't say that."

"I mean it."

"It's too late."

"Why do you keep saying that?"

When she speaks again her voice is dispassionate. "I'm moving out, Connor."

"Where will you move to?"

"Look, I've got to go now."

"Don't go. Wait. Call me on my line — just for a minute."

"Why?"

"I just . . . please."

"I've really got to go."

"Please, Phil—"

"Goodbye, Connor."

And she does go, back into that lurid void which I roam in my sleeplessness where she trills her song of lust beneath a man without a face.

DINNER AT "21"

Brooke couldn't handle the farewell repast, finding neither the concepts of (1) eating nor (2) family irresistible. I have dutifully dragged myself to this final Station of the Cross: the 'rents are leaving in the morning. Dad is subdued and chagrined after his performance yesterday. His hands are shaking, although he cheers up in the downstairs saloon after hearty personal greetings from Bruce, the manager, and Joseph, our waiter. He sips black coffee, spilling as much in his saucer as he manages to bring to his lips. Doing my best to uphold the family dishonor, I drink Bloody Bulls.

"Your grandfather used to sit at this booth." This statement is directed at me, the young master, apparent heir to the high regard of a third generation of "21" waiters and captains. "Used to sit right in that corner banquette over there, they'd beat him to the table with an extra-dry Beefeater martini, straight up with three olives." My father's voice is full of sentimental masculine pride, as if spending half your life on your butt drinking martinis were a tremendous dynastic accomplishment. "Whenever we couldn't find him, we'd call here first. He took me here after I got into Williams and bought me my first official drink."

Thoughts about my grandfather: smart enough to sniff the crash of '29 coming and pull out with a couple million, which really *was* a couple million in those days, but not smart enough to realize that all his hard work, financial acumen and shady dealing would result merely in his son's being debilitated by the patrimony, which said cripple would pretty much squander.

"What's wrong, sweetie," Mom asks, after Dad wobbles off to the bathroom. Ditsy as she is, I forget sometimes how acute Mom can be. "Has she left you, Connor?"

All at once my chest is heaving. When she asked me about Philomena earlier, I tried to dissemble cheerfully, chattering about her trip, her career, our plans.

"I'm so sorry, honey." Sitting beside me on the banquette my mother hugs me and wipes my face. "I haven't done a very good job of preparing you for anything, have I?"

Even in this shattered mood, I'm able to laugh at the notion of Mom as a trainer.

"I remember when you were born," she says, "just before the big freeze. You wouldn't remember, of course, but the temperature hit twenty degrees. And your father was out working through the night, spraying the groves when my contractions started. You were a breech birth, did I ever tell you? And it was a long terrible night for me and for your father out in the groves. And we were in the hospital almost a week. When I came home, all along the road I could see the damage—the leaves turning brown and falling off, but the fruit still hanging on the naked trees like Christmas-tree balls. And when we came around the corner from the Jenkses' to our land I saw the leaves were still green. The ice had saved the trees. And I suddenly realized it could have been different; that I might've lost you. And I remember at that moment wanting so much to be able to protect you from everything that was cold and unpleasant." She stroked my hair. Her eyes were glazed, but for once I felt she was truly looking at me. "And I'm so sorry that I can't." For just a minute, I find perfect sanctuary in the dark softness of my mother's breasts.

Then Dad returns, bringing the world and the sad distance of family life with him.

HOUSE CALL

The buzzer summons me from the blissful oblivion I have somehow achieved on the couch, my first real sleep in several days. Ignoring it is not a luxury available to someone like myself hoping desperately for a miracle. I leap from the couch and stumble to the door, rubbing my neck. Imagine my surprise and chagrin to discover Dr. Halliwell on my doorstep. It takes me a moment to recognize him, though. The green hospital scrubs under his anorak finally clinch it.

"I just happened to be, well, actually, I was over at St. Vincent's and I thought I'd drop by."

Unable to summon a defensive strategy, I usher him in. Despite the fact that I think he's a dweeb, I am mortified to look at the apartment through his eyes. Sent the cleaning lady away last week because I was trying to sleep and because I was embarrassed even for *her* to see the wreckage, with the result that it has grown and compounded itself as rapidly as the interest on an unpaid VISA balance. If I could wish away any one element of the debris at this moment, it would be the dead soldiers, the beer, Absolut and Jack Daniel's bottles that suddenly seem so very numerous indeed. I realize, of course, that dirty clothing and towels do not belong in the living room, where they detract from the air quality and overall ambience. And how could any one person read, let alone own, so many newspapers and magazines? Well, I am a literate slob, at least. The best that can otherwise be said is that there aren't a lot of dirty plates, since I haven't eaten much. Just a couple of pizza boxes spread around the few available surfaces, like accent pieces.

"Little party last night," I mumble. "Few friends over to watch the game."

"Oh, that's very, that must have been . . ."

"Listen, it's a little messy here. You want to step out for a drink?" I grab my jacket from the back of the couch and push him back out the way he came.

"I didn't mean to disturb you."

"Actually," I lie, "I'd just finished writing a piece."

"I enjoyed your article on . . . I've forgotten her name. Actress."

"You must be thinking of my ode to Cortney Thorne Smith." If Doug were anyone else I would know he was mocking me. The sad thing is I believe he means it. Perhaps Doug admired that poignant passage in which Cortney admitted that she'd always been ashamed of her body and almost had (gasp!) breast reduction. At any rate, he is reminding me however inadvertently of the absurdity of my existence, which does not improve my general mood.

We pass a black transvestite in a silver-fox coat trudging up Washington on his way to work. Blow jobs for the hubbies in Cherokees; watch out for the baby seat. Doug looks back at the trannie and I wonder if he is shocked.

"I think I treated him for hepatitis a couple of months ago."

I'm—what? Surprised, impressed. Small world, though Doug's world is larger than I'd imagined.

Albert King's guitar piercing the frigid evening air outside as I usher Doug into Automatic Slims, my local drinketeria, which is sparsely populated at this early hour. What is this hour? Whatever happened to my Swatch? And who was the actor I once interviewed who confessed that the best thing about fame was that he no longer needed to wear an expensive watch to get respect?

Is the sun over the yardarm yet? My father, before he tucks into his first drink of the day, likes to announce that it is. I've never stopped to ask what this means. Should I ask Doug? But he doesn't look like a sailor. So I order a Bloody Mary, which is appropriate anytime, while Doug settles for a club soda and lime.

"On duty at eight," he explains. Otherwise, you know, he'd *really* be getting down, doing shooters and Mad Dogging all over the place. Maybe I should take him up to Hogs and Heifers, where Julia Roberts dances on the bar.

A SERIOUS TALK

"Listen, I don't mean to be . . . it's just that I'm a little, not worried, but let's say *concerned* about Brooke."

"In what way?" While I'm not unconcerned about Brooke myself—I'm terrified—I'm not necessarily prepared to confide in this relative stranger.

"Well, there's her . . . she doesn't really eat. I think she has a problem, a potential problem, in this area. And some days she can hardly drag herself out of bed." An awkward pause—as if remembering he has just awakened her brother in the p.m. Aha! A family trait. "I see some . . . let's just say, *depressive* tendencies." He sips his soda pensively. "And I thought maybe you could, I thought if we could just discuss it. . . ."

Part of me would like to reach out to this man, to tell him that I share his worries and it's breaking my heart. But it's *my* heart, and Brooke is *my* sister. "Brooke's always gone through these phases," I explain. "She gets a little weird, stops eating for a while, then she wakes up one morning and she's fine again."

"I think it's a little worse than that," he says, as forcefully as I've ever heard him say anything.

"She'll be all right," I insist.

"This may seem like, I don't mean to overstep any bounds, but is there any history of this kind of thing in your family?"

I could tell him about my paternal grandmother, who once tried to drown a certain evil spirit who by her account was in possession of my father's five-year-old body, and who was shipped up to a bucolic institution in Connecticut every couple of years for what they called nerves. As Irish Catholics, my father's side has done an excellent job of acquiring the neurasthenic traits of ancient Wasp pedigree while preserving the traditional failings associated with the old sod. And then there's Mom's Faulknerian family—completely batshit.

But I say, "Nothing particularly comes to mind."

"The family doesn't seem to be functioning . . . quite as supportively as it might."

"We can take care of ourselves."

"I hate to bring this up, but your father just exposed himself in public yesterday."

"I didn't say we weren't eccentric."

At least he didn't cut it off, like some of Doug's acquaintances.

He stares into my eyes for the first time that I can remember, his face hardening into a mask of judgment. "You're not the only one who loves Brooke."

I realize that I am being a complete asshole. And I am almost ready to yield, to try to behave like a decent person, when Doug stands up and lays a five-dollar bill on the bar. "Well, thanks," he says. "I better get up to the hospital."

"I'll see you," I say, hating myself just a little more than usual.

BROOKE CHECK

She's watching the Bosnian War Crimes Tribunal on Court TV.

"Let's go get a bite."

"I'll bet that's exactly what this murderer said right after he eviscerated a Bosnian Muslim in front of his family."

"It was just a thought."

She continues to stare at the screen, where the defendant, wearing headphones and penal pajamas, listens to the proceedings with an expression more bored than belligerent.

"Your boyfriend came to visit me," I say.

"You're always pissing and moaning about the fashionable people you claim you're forced to associate with," she says in an even, uninflected tone, still staring at the TV. "But I'm afraid you've become one of them."

"What does that have to do with Mad Dog?"

"You make fun of him because he's not cool, because he doesn't have an ego that sticks out six feet in front of him like an erection when he walks down the street." She directs at me a look of cool and brutal appraisal. "I hate like hell to say it, but right now Doug's a better person than you are, Connor. Last night at the end of Doug's shift an eighty-three-year-old woman came into the emergency room with her lungs full of fluid, and she said to Doug, 'I know I'm dying, don't tell me I'm not.' And he told her it was true. And she asked him if he would stay with her while she died and he said he would. And he did. He sat with that woman for two hours and talked to her and held her hand until she slipped away. . . ."

Which is what I do, eventually—slip away. Had I come to check up on her, or on myself?

L U N C H   A T   " 4 4 "

"Sorry I'm late. Listen, I was at Chaos this weekend and the weirdest thing happened." Tina Christian pauses and looks longingly at the distant row of banquettes upon which sprawl the dukes and duchesses of the periodical publishing realm. "Next time," she says, "let me make the reservation." Vis-à-vis our table, which is virtually outside the castle walls. I stand to hold her chair, the chivalrous McKnight.

"So this Latina babe comes up and starts schmoozing me. I thought she looked familiar. She's kind of cute in a Janet Jackson sort of way, but she was with some very tough looking chicks, they were like a pack or something. Then she starts asking me about you. At first it seems real innocent, but then she starts asking me if I'm your girlfriend and I get this funny vibe and finally I'm, like, whoa, wait a minute, this is that crazy bitch who sent you the naked picture. Which by the way we all enjoyed. But before I realize that's who she is I thought she was a friend of yours and we just kind of started talking. She seemed kind of suspicious about who I was so I was like 'Hey, I *wish*, Connor's a really cool guy but he's totally devoted to his girlfriend.' I mean, for all I know she could have been a friend of Philomena's. So then she's like 'Oh, yeah, I hear she's really great,' and I'm like 'Yeah, for a model she's actually okay.' If you really want to know, I said she was great. Which she is, I've never had a problem with Philomena except that it's kind of hard to be in the room with her because on her worst day she makes me feel like the basset hound standing next to a whippet. Anyway, I told this girl that you weren't a typical modelfucker and that you guys were like this old married couple, and she starts asking all these questions which eventually turn nasty. And finally I realize she's some kind of psycho, so of course I get out of there. I mean, who *is* this chick?"

"I don't know. She could be my next girlfriend." Thus you proceed to share your romantic woes with Tina, hoping for a little feminine advice.

"Not good," she says, worrying a breadstick with her teeth.

"What would you do?"

"I find in these situations the only thing *to* do is sleep with somebody else as soon as possible. Even if you don't really feel like it, at least you have the illusion of revenge. And having someone else's scent on you immediately makes you more attractive to the injuring party." Then, staring into the distance: "God, I've got to find out who's cutting Tina Brown's hair."

A   F L A M E

To: Scribbler@aol.com
From: Jenrod@inch.com
Subject: Modelfuckers

So now I know why you didn't even bother to show up at Chaos and why you are so high and migty about helping a person whose just looking for some career advice and a friendly shoulder to "lean on." Or even maybe, who knows? See what develops between them? Someone who might be a soulmate instead of just some pretty face although not to blow my own horn lots of people say I'm way prettier than most of the socalled models in your stupid magazine. Just because your girlfriend is a "top fashion model" I suppose you think you're better than other people. Speaking of Swell Heads I'll bet she has a real beach ball between her ears—full of air! I suppose you don't know that most models are really lesbians! What do you think they do standing around halfnaked in dressing rooms all day? You better believe their noses aren't so high up in the air then! But maybe your one of those sickos who likes to watch. Some day may be you'll learn the meaning of the expression "beauty is only skin deep." And by then it will be too late. There is another expression of mine—be nice to the people you meet on the way up because you will meet them again on your way down. And may be that will be me waving to you from my limo when you are drunken in the gutter. And where will your anorexic PUSSYLICKING girlfriend be then?

I'm not one of those people who believes everything they hear I believe in giving people the benefit of the doubt until proven guilty even OJ Simpson. So I'm basically giving you one more chance to do the polite thing and at least have the guts to say Hey sorry I stood you up.

INTERVIEW WITH A VAMPIRE

Still no word from Chip Ralston, but I have scheduled an interview with his friend Jason Townes. Chip's publicist booked it through Jason's manager. Jason's staying at the Four Seasons, in town to promote his new movie, and I'm slotted in for 10 p.m. By all accounts he is a night person. I consider calling to confirm, but decide my chances might be better if I don't give him a chance to reconsider. Sometime around 9 I fall asleep in front of the television, waking up at 11:30 to the closing music of an ancient *Cheers* episode. Running for a cab, I forget both my notebook and my tape recorder, arriving in the lobby at 10 to 12. I pick up the house phone and ask for Stanley Kowalski, the name under which Townes has registered, having waited for someone to compare him to Brando since he was in summer stock.

"And who may I say is calling?" asks the house operator. After many minutes she comes back on the line to say she's sorry, Mr. Kowalski is not available. I have an appointment, I insist: McKnight, Connor. Writer. Another interlude of Muzak—not Rod, thank God—before she comes back on and gives me a room number.

Upstairs, I knock several times. "Hey, what's up." The kid who finally admits me looks like a midwestern collegiate athlete, closely shorn and blandly handsome, except for a prominent gold nose ring. He shakes my hand. "I'm Tab." My comprehensive research indicates that Townes travels with an entourage of high school buddies. This is sometimes taken, in the popular press, as a sign of what a loyal, down-to-earth guy he is—as opposed to, say, someone who needs a lot of help lugging his ego around.

Inside, it's hard to see for the dimness, the atmosphere thick with smoke and a vague menace. Jason Townes is sitting on a couch in a white terry-cloth robe, staring at the television. A plump, voluptuous brunette in a tiny pink negligee is beside him, rubbing his shoulders. As I approach tentatively, Jason rises and extends his hand, looking sincere, if somewhat fucked up.

"Hey, how are you, dude? Catch a seat." Tab sits down beside the young woman and squeezes her ample breast, then leans over and uses an American Express platinum card to separate a huge line from a pile of white powder on the coffee table. He snorts the line through a hundred. All very eighties.

A buff young skinhead, who appears at first to be wearing a loud, colorful Hawaiian shirt, emerges from one of the rooms, towel wrapped around his waist. In fact he is shirtless, his torso adorned with a mosaic of tattoos, the sweaty tesserae composed of skulls, dragons and naked women. Toting his own rolled bill, he leans over and snorts a line, clutching his towel modestly.

I introduce myself. Jason, watching himself on the screen, does not look up. The tattooed man nods and says, "Kirk."

"Kirk just got off the road," says he of the nose ring, "with the Red Hot Chilis."

"That was some wild shit," says Kirk. "Talk about pussy, this one chick offered to let us pierce her clit."

"Yeah, well," says Tab, "that's like, Jason, man—one time this rich bitch once offered him twenty-five big ones for a locket of pubic hair."

"No way."

"The raddest," says Jason, still looking at the screen, "was that kid who killed himself onstage when the Cure was playing in Brazil. Now that's fucking commitment."

Kirk says, "I know this dope dealer—"

"We're shocked," says Jason.

"This dealer claims he knows a guy who has Errol Flynn's dick in like a jar. Supposedly it was secretly cut off and preserved in like whatever you call it. Says the asking price is a million."

"See, I should be charging *you*," Jason says to the girl, who is surely someone's sixteen-year-old Sicilian cousin from Queens. "Mine should be worth at least a hundred large."

"Then you'd have to be nice to me," the girl says.

"That reminds me, somebody was telling me this story," Jason says, but he is distracted by his own image on-screen. "I love this part." He points. "Did that stunt myself."

"He did," Tab says. "Director says, 'Jason, get out of the car, let's put the double in.' J. says, 'No way man. Just watch this shit.' "

Howls of amazed appreciation are provoked as the car sails off an overpass and lands on top of another moving vehicle.

"That," says Kirk, "is some styling roadwork."

Without looking away from the screen, Jason says, "So what's the pitch? You got three minutes."

"Pitch?" I say.

"For the flick." He looks at me, finally. "Aren't you a writer?"

"Actually, I'm here to interview you about Chip Ralston."

"Speaking of morons," says Kirk.

"Chip?" The girl looks up. "I think he's sexy."

Jason raises his eyebrows, then suddenly shoots his hand up between her legs. She squirms and squeals like a child being tickled.

"Chip's all right," Jason allows. "Hell, he's my best friend. He's down with me. Nothing wrong with Chip that a personality implant wouldn't fix."

Tab laughs—a throaty, barking sound that Jason seems to appreciate.

"You shouldn't say that about your friend," the brunette whines.

"Personality implant," says Jason, "and an ego reduction."

"That's a good one, J."

"Fucking guy, he's so clueless, he can't even take a piss without calling his psychic. Wait, now I remember that story," says Jason. "Chip said in an interview he liked van Gogh. Like he'd probably just heard the name from whoever was directing his latest picture. A week later he gets a fucking ear in the mail. Some *ho* sliced off her fucking ear just to show her devotion to the great Chip Ralston. Jesus, I fucking hate the way he shot me in this scene," Jason concludes, pointing again. "Look at this, rewind it. Fucking guy couldn't direct a Pampers commercial."

Tab barks and wallops his thigh.

"All this is *off the record*," Jason says to me. "Everything so far. And all this—" He waves his arm around the immediate vicinity of the couch. "You want some food, something to drink?" He gestures toward the huge buffet table in the middle of the room: striped orange shrimp and pearl-gray caviar, pâtés and melting mousses, cheeses and breads, sushi and sashimi. Somehow it all looks hyper-real, as luridly unappetizing in the murky funk of the suite as the lacquered plastic models in Japanese restaurant windows. More than slightly nauseous making. The bar is more to my liking, Cristal and an '85 Montrachet chilled in silver buckets; a fine selection of white and brown liquors, with all the mixers.

I taste the wine, probably excellent if one hadn't been smoking and drinking for five days straight and had something in the way of taste buds left. Instead, I pour myself a large tumbler of Absolut. Aiming for a chair, I almost step on something, which on examination turns out to be a used condom, glistening like something recently living and freshly killed and skinned on the shaggy savanna of the carpet.

"Ow, that hurts." The young lady exclaims, trying to extract the star's hand from between her legs.

"Show the nice man your tits," Jason says, withdrawing his hand, sniffing it absently.

Shrugging demurely, she caresses the straps of her negligee over her shoulders, down her plump arms, revealing an abundance, a positive surplus, of blue-veined, white breast meat and dark, protuberant silver-dollar-sized nipples. Like the buffet, it seems a bit much.

"Nice, huh?"

"Great," I say.

"Right on. So you're a fucking journalist."

"Not really. I'd hardly—"

"I thought you were this screenwriter my fucking agent was hooking me up with. He, like, won an Oscar a few years ago. He's pretty famous. What's his name?" Jason looks at Tab.

"Steve something," Jason's friend concludes after a long pause and another line. "Or maybe Victor."

"Something like that. Wasn't he supposed to come up and

pitch? Maybe you guys could corroborate. Couple of wordjockeys and all." He chuckles, seeming to contemplate the absurdity and drudgery of the logocentic realm, where scriveners scribble and toil, huffing and puffing like stevedores as they lift and carry big Latinate verbs and portmanteau nouns while Jason and his kind get all the pussy. He takes the rolled bill and sticks it in the mound of white powder.

"Actually, I am kind of working on a screenplay." God, did I actually say that? Without even the excuse of having consumed drugs? Disgusted with myself even before I finish the sentence.

Jason moans. "So's the fucking guy who cleans my pool." He turns to the girl. "Hey, I'll bet *you're* working on a goddamn screenplay."

"I have these thoughts sometimes," she says. "I write them down in this journal."

He looks at me. "What did I tell you?"

A very nude young man suddenly appears in the hall from another part of the suite, his slick, semierect penis bobbing absurdly like a dowsing rod.

"My turn," says Kirk, rising eagerly from the couch. A beautiful woman in a white terry-cloth robe materializes in the hallway, wafting toward us like a dream.

"I need another five hundred if I'm staying," she says, seeing me a moment after I recognize her.

"Kirk, get the money from my dresser," Jason says. Then, "What, you two know each other?"

Pallas is actually blushing. All that I will salvage from this encounter is the notion that she, too, can blush. I don't know why I care; I don't know exactly what kind of faith I thought I had deposited in trust with this woman who never promised me anything except a dance and a good view of her excellent breasts for twenty dollars—who threw in a blow job, gratis.

I'm not quite shocked, just thoroughly deflated.

"You want to go first?" Jason asks me. "Kirk can wait. He's already been in there once tonight."

"Twice," Kirk corrects.

"Don't worry about the bucks, it's on me," Jason says. "She's good, dude."

"I'm sure she is," I say. "I just remembered I have to go home and finish reading Saint Augustine's *Confessions.*"

"Yeah, well, whatever," says Jason. "Hey, Kirk, where's the remote? Rewind that part back to the two shot." For all his careless generosity Jason Townes has forgotten me long before I have reached the door.

"Hey, that's my bill," he tells someone. "That's how you get hepatitis, sharing rolled-up bills."

A RARE PERSONAL APPEARANCE

When I return to my apartment Jeremy is leaning against my door, pressing the buzzer. He appears uncharacteristically inebriated.

"Are you acquainted with any contract killers?" he asks.

Pacing my living room floor, he pauses to survey the rubble. "Jesus, I think you've been robbed."

"Actually, I have been."

"Join the fucking club." He fumbles in his pockets, hands me a note:

> *I'm afraid we've become far too fond of Ronald to give him up. But perhaps we might be persuaded at a later date. Our apologies for any inconvenience this may have caused you. Sincerely—Edie Jamison.*

"Taped to the fucking door. House empty. Nobody home." It seems, as he finally explains it, that Jeremy has just returned from a trip to New Jersey where, by prior arrangement, he was to exchange four thousand dollars in actual U.S. currency for the terrier. "And she has the gall, did I tell you this, to name Sean—who already has a name that he knows and responds to—she has the fucking temerity to rename him *Ronald*—like Ronald fucking McDonald!"

When I smash my fist into the wall, Jeremy stops to catch his breath. He ambles over to examine the indentation in the plaster. "That must have hurt," he says.

ANOTHER LITERARY MYSTERY SOLVED

Later, we're drinking at the Whitehorse Tavern amidst the usual collection of students, hard-core locals and tourists visiting the shrine where Dylan Thomas drank his last.

"I'm thinking of flying to L.A.," I say.

"Better you than me. Ever heard the joke, studio decides to make *David Copperfield*, studio head says, 'What about a script?' Exec says, 'We're thinking William Goldman, Robert Towne.' Studio head says, 'What about the author? He tied up on another project, or what?' " Jeremy halts drunkenly. "Actually, that's a true story."

"Actually, I don't even know if she's in L.A."

"Wait, quiet, this is my song," he commands, as the lugubrious opening chords of "It Wouldn't Have Made Any Difference" ooze from the jukebox. Unself-conscious for once in his life, Jeremy sings along while the tears well in my eyes: *"It wouldn't have made any difference, / if you loved me . . . / You just didn't love me."*

Popular songs become profound when we are wounded in love. I fire up a cigarette. Smoke gets in your eyes.

When the song ends, Jeremy says, "It's not the same playing it at home as hearing it in a bar, on a jukebox. The smoke, the draft beer, the company of all these fucking losers, the tinny, low-fidelity speakers competing against the obnoxious voices of one's fellow drinkers. The gritty poignancy of it all. That's how certain songs are meant to be heard. Jukeboxes are time machines for the bereft."

Jeremy tosses his long mane, unconsciously evoking quivers from a table of NYU coeds on the other side of the room. It should be counted to Jeremy's credit that he is generally unaware of the interest he excites in the opposite sex, though an ill-wisher might chalk up this obliviousness to self-absorption.

"Listen," he says, "think about this." Pausing for effect.

"I'm listening."

"Holly Golightly and Sally Bowles."

"Please, enough sluts for one night."

"I was reading what's-his-name's biography of Capote when it came to me. Capote was a big admirer of Isherwood and they eventually became friends. So I picked up *The Berlin Stories* and then went back and reread *Breakfast at Tiffany's*. No question, Holly is an American clone of Sally Bowles, right down to the unconvincingly heterosexual pal. A total rip-off. I mean, it's practically plagiarism."

WHAT PHILOMENA BRIGGS HAS IN COMMON WITH HOLLY GOLIGHTLY AND SALLY BOWLES

When Connor fails to swoon with excitement, Jeremy asks, "What do you mean enough sluts for one night? Did Philomena come back?"

Connor has a sudden dark inspiration: "Do you know something about Phil that I don't?" By now imagining himself fully prepared for, even expecting, the worst. "Or are you just trying to cheer me up?"

"What would I know?"

"I don't know, is she giving blow jobs in the Lincoln Tunnel? Sleeping with quadrupeds? I mean, am I deluded in thinking that she was faithful, that we had a fairly decent relationship, that this latest . . . *thing* is, I don't know—*uncharacteristic?*"

Jeremy hesitates, inhales and exhales in the manner prescribed by the Zen masters. "Listen, I've been meaning to tell you. There's this story in the new collection called 'Model Behavior.' It's *fiction*, okay. A fictive narrative. But I wanted to tell you before you read it."

"Tell me what?"

"It's basically a story about illusion and reality, about the worship of false idols. Part of the overall metaphoric construct of the collection—the claustrophobic madness of the city." He looks at me hopefully, as if to say, *Who could dispute the validity of such a theme?* "It's kind of about a writer and a model." He sighs. "It's about this guy who has an affair with his best friend's girlfriend. Which could appear to you, in a paranoid moment, to be based on real events. But I swear to you it never happened. It's what Roth calls *The Counterlife*. Basically the what-if version, the might-have-been version. I just wanted to tell you that before you read it."

Sensing Connor's disbelief, he becomes indignant. "I mean, I don't even know why I'm explaining this, you know the difference between fiction and nonfiction. Okay, sure, hate me for my fantasy, but I just didn't want you to think . . . you know what I mean."

He takes a long swallow of beer, watching Connor over the top of his mug.

For all the discounts he has made in his own self-esteem in recent years, Connor never imagined Philomena to be interested in anyone but himself.

"What happened?"

"I told you—nothing. The story's just a projection."

"This is me, Jeremy. I know all about your so-called fiction."

"It's a possible world."

"Jesus, Jeremy."

"Nothing really happened. Sure, maybe I wanted to. . . . It was nothing." He sighs again, placing his mug carefully on its coaster. "You were in L.A. I don't know, a year ago. We just, I ran into her at the movies and then we went out for a drink."

"A drink."

"I was telling her about a book, I don't know, something in the movie reminded me of Jim Salter, and we went back to my place so I could give her the book."

"Oh, *right*. Salter. Nice. *A Sport and a Pastime*, perhaps."

He shrugs. "Yeah, well."

"I can't believe this."

"I'm not trying to make excuses, okay? I guess I knew . . . I guess I felt a certain amorous—"

"What happened?"

"We kissed. Once. That's it."

Connor is reeling. *"Kissed?"* He wants to see the picture clearly, in color, so he can suffer its every detail. "Who started it?"

"I don't know, it just kind of happened."

"What did?"

"One minute we're talking about *A Sport and a Pastime* and then we were . . . we kissed. For a minute. For less than a minute. I mean, we stopped before . . . you know. Before anything."

"No, tell me. I don't know. I wasn't there. Did she take off her clothes? Did you feel her tits? Stick your finger in her twat?"

Jeremy is trying to shush his friend while the bartender scrutinizes him with a constabulary air.

"Nothing happened. We *stopped*, okay?"

"Who stopped?"

"Who cares? I don't know."

"Who stopped? And who didn't want to stop?"

"Connor, give it up. You don't need this."

"Yes, I do. *You* give it up."

"*I* stopped, all right? Are you happy now? *I* did."

"My friend."

"That's right."

It is a curious dilemma Connor's impaled upon, trying to decide whether he would rather be betrayed by his best friend or his lover. His former lover. His lost lover.

"I'm sorry, Connor, I've beaten myself up till my conscience is black and blue. It would've been easier for me to tell you. Look, it could've been worse. It was nothing, really. We were drunk. It was just a kiss, that's all. And later out of guilt and speculation and because it's what I do as a writer, I embellished it into a story."

"A story which everybody will think is true."

A DAZE

Everything in the room seems to be wrapped in a skein of gauze. You feel dissociated from the physical environment, as if you were high. You feel Jeremy's hand on your shoulder, the first time you can remember him initiating physical contact. You always have noticed the little things—Jeremy's eccentricities, for instance, or your own little mood swings—but you now realize that you have failed to take note of the big things. You have suffered a chronic and massive failure of awareness. And it occurs to you that inattention might, cumulatively, spread over years, be as great a crime as infidelity.

"Don't worry about *everybody*," he says, regaining his customary belligerence. "I mean, who's everybody? How many readers do I have? For that matter, how many friends do you have?"

"One less." Even as you say this, you know it's melodramatic, and that you will forgive Jeremy. But for now you must follow the customary forms of indignation. You stand up, throw a twenty down on the bar, a radical gesture, given how few of them are left in your possession.

"She knew about that actress in L.A.," Jeremy shouts as you retreat.

Ah, that.

Outside, the cold air helps jar you into a belated sense of alertness. You start up the street, reflecting on each step you take, as in walking meditation. Such is your glowering sense of menace that a ragged mendicant starts to approach and then dodges away from you.

TINA TO THE RESCUE

You stalk west to Washington Street. You want to be in a small loud room full of strangers who can barely hear themselves speak above the music, consuming first- *and* secondhand smoke, all the fucking smoke you can wrap your lungs around. Back to Automatic Slims, jam-packed from the bar to the windows. Adding your own body to the fray, you can't help feeling that it is the oldest in the room. You might not have noticed last week, or even yesterday, but no one in the place looks much over twenty. And they all seem too fucking happy, as if they didn't know how shitty their lives were about to become, once they graduate from Columbia or Sarah Lawrence or NYU Law School and learn that the hangovers only get worse.

When exactly did you lose that feeling of invulnerability and infinite promise, your belief in both yourself and the abundance of time? You didn't really notice its leaving, but tonight you can say with certainty that it's gone.

A blond flag on a black stick: Tina Christian emerges from the men's room, pinching her nose, wrapping you in a brittle embrace.

"Connor, I am *so* glad to see you, you look like shit. I'm just on my way to Spy Bar. You can be my date."

"I'm not very good company."

"I can't afford to be picky. At least you're taller than me." She tugs me toward the door. "Have you talked to Jeremy?"

"I just left him."

She stops to wave at someone behind you. "*Where?* Did he mention me? God, I have *got* to talk to him. I am *so* not proud of myself but I was, like, I couldn't help it. Kevin was being such an asshole and I was so pissed that I told him about sleeping with Jeremy. I think I must have been drunk. Plus I was a little pissed at Jeremy because he hadn't called me. I know, I know . . . I just feel *terrible* about it. . . ."

DAYBREAK

Sleep is out of the question. At five-fifteen the red light pulses through the blinds and I am sober despite my best efforts to stupefy myself, my virtue nominally intact despite Tina's best efforts. I sent her away when I finally realized she was making me feel worse instead of better. Now I sit up and spread the slats; they're loading a body in the back of the ambulance. The sheet stretches all the way over the lump of the head.

Earlier I had bobbed in Tina's frothy wake, following her first to Spy Bar, then to Chaos, because we heard from a friend of hers that Chip Ralston was supposed to show up there. Chip was not present, but Tina introduced me in the bathroom to a friend of hers who claimed that he'd sold him some ketamine last week and who offered to sell me a ring that used to belong to River Phoenix. "If you're really interested," he said, "I know a guy whose cousin worked at the funeral parlor. Dude scooped a handful of ashes from the urn, he's selling them by the gram." Searching the pocked face for a glimmer of irony, I listened to Tina puking in one of the stalls.

GOOD MORNING: A FAX!

Dear Connor:
     Finally got hold of Brooke last night, told her about Christmas. She said she understood, but she sounded a little manic to me. What's going on? I'm counting on you to look after the girl. If anything happens to her you will wish I had drowned you back when you were six.
     I have a meeting in New York a few days before Christmas so maybe we can all go down to Florida together and spend a day there before I go on to Freeport.

Love,
Corvetta

WORD FROM RALSTON'S CAMP

Evening: I'm at my computer checking various Web sites— http://www.starzzz.com; www.hollyword.com—when the phone rings; my caller ID shows an incoming call from Los Angeles.
     "Hello?" I start jotting down the number, a 310.
     "Hello, could I please speak to Colin McNeal?"
     "Would you settle for Connor McKnight?"
     "Oh, sure. This is Cherie Smith. Chip Ralston's assistant? Chip just wanted me to tell you that he's changed his mind about the article. He decided he won't be able to do it after all."
     "Are you kidding?"
     "He just told me to tell you is all."
     "Excuse me," I say. "Do you think I could speak to him?"

"I'm sorry, but he's really busy right now."

"It's not that I'm dying to write this article, but I don't have enough money in my checking account to pay my half of next month's rent, let alone my missing girlfriend's half."

"I'm sorry, but I'm just doing my job. Well, have a nice day. Bye."

I'm not about to give up that easily. Now I have the number. Out to get a pack of smokes, practicing my imitation of Jason Townes, trying to reproduce his famous dusky tone in order to get past the assistant and speak directly to Ralston, my prey, the bastard.

"Jason Townes here." No, not quite. "Hi, Jason calling. Can I talk to Chip." Close. "Hi, it's Jason," I say, shivering at the corner of Twelfth and Hudson. "Jason Townes."

"Yeah, and I'm Michelle Pfeiffer," says the young black woman walking her dog behind me.

Back in my apartment I smoke two cigarettes to abrade my voice, wait fifteen minutes, then call back the magic number inscribed on my notepad.

"Hello?" says the familiar voice. "Hello? Who is this?"

"Phil?"

"Connor?"

"What are you doing there," I ask, when I finally find my voice, though the answer seems obvious enough, if somewhat incredible.

"How did you—"

"Does that *matter*?" I say. "I mean, you're asking *me* how I . . . Jesus. I can't believe this is happening."

"I didn't want to hurt your feelings."

"You didn't want to hurt my feelings? *That's* why you're fucking Chip Ralston—to spare my feelings? What would you do if you actually *wanted* to grind me under your pointy little heel and crush my spirit beyond repair?"

"I mean, that's why I didn't want you to know."

"And *that's* why he blew off the stupid fucking interview?"

"Connor, you could hardly write objectively about him under the circumstances."

"I didn't *know* the circumstances."

"Well, you would have." After a pause she adds, "*Hard Copy* caught us leaving Morton's last night. It'll probably run tonight."

"I'm getting on a plane right now."

"Connor, don't. It's over. Anyway, we're going to Montana this afternoon."

"Montana?"

"Chip has a place outside Livingston. We're going to spend some time there."

"It must be just . . . *lovely*."

"I told you I wanted a simpler life."

"*Simpler?* You're going to Livingston fucking Montana with Chip fucking Ralston. Do you have any idea what a cliché that is? I've got it in my computer. 'CTRL, *Montana cliché*.' It's not simple. It's just stupid."

She is silent on the other end; as for me, I can hardly speak. Finally I say, "This is a joke, right?"

"Connor, these things happen. You know? It's nobody's fault."

"Chip Ralston?"

"I can understand your being upset."

"It's pathetic."

"Don't make me say things you don't want to hear."

"He's a fucking midget, Phil."

"Don't worry about that, Connor. Chip's a giant where it counts, thank you very much."

I slam down the phone and regret doing so immediately. Scooping up an Imari porcelain frog—one of Philomena's prized possessions—I hurl it against the wall, where it shatters predictably. We bought it at a flea market in Kyoto and I remember wondering what would happen to it, the first durable object we had ever purchased together: Would it become a stitch binding us together? Would we look at it ten years, twenty years, hence and remember? Afterward we went back to the Ryokan in the hills to the west of town, where the deep cedar tub was steaming in anticipation of our arrival, blue-and-white striped robes laid out on the black-bordered tatami mats. What would I give to go back, if I could? Would I relive it all to this moment, with foreknowledge? Or would I drown the bitch right there in the tub?

For the next twenty minutes I call the number on my pad, filling Chip's answering tape with expletives and entreaties. After the fifth call the number rings continuously.

I'm trying to imagine how to live with myself for the next thirty years when the buzzer goes off.

MORE GRIEF

Jeremy stands in the doorway. Wild eyed, he brushes past me into the apartment.

"You and your fucking girlfriend!"

"I just talked to her."

"Who?"

"Philomena."

"Don't even mention the name."

"What," I say. "What did you hear?"

"Read all about it." He's waving a newspaper in his hand.

"Philomena's in the paper?"

"Oh, she's in the paper all right."

To Connor it seems perfectly reasonable that his girlfriend's treachery should be exposed in the *New York Times*. With trembling hand, he takes it, folded open to the middle of the C section, and sees Jeremy's picture glowering handsomely beneath the headline: GLIB DEPRESSIVES ON PARADE. Confused, he says, "It's a book review."

"It's not a fucking book review," Jeremy shouts. "It's a knife in my heart."

Connor reads further:

> Jeremy Green's first collection earned the author a solid if
> modest reputation as a literary craftsman possessed of a darkly
> humorous vision. Since then he has been photographed at
> trendy gatherings in the company of fashion models and

cavorting in the company of such movie stars as Liam Neeson and Natasha Richardson. "Walled-In," his new collection, seems less like the product of an original artistic vision than a self-conscious display of glitzy urban angst. . . .

"Three years of work, a lifetime's apprenticeship to my fucking craft . . ." A savage kick sends a sofa cushion flying across the room. "Does that count? Dragged kicking and screaming to *one* lousy party, thrown out of *one* celebrity watering hole—and now I'm a whore? 'Glitzy urban angst'? '*Cavorting*' with movie stars?"

Although Connor has difficulty concentrating, he can see that the rest of the review follows syllogistically from the lead. He asks himself, If given the choice of having Phil back or else rescinding Jeremy's review . . . and in so doing comes up against the limits of altruism. "She's run off with Chip Ralston," he says.

"Fuck Chip Ralston. And fuck Philomena. Fuck all of you."

Not knowing what else to do, Connor pours out two tumblers of vodka and places one of them in Jeremy's hand.

"I can imagine—"

"Nobody can imagine," Jeremy barks. "Nobody who hasn't been here."

"It's not that bad," Connor says. "I mean, I've seen worse."

Jeremy looks at the glass as if he'd never seen one before, then hurls it across the room. Rising and bolting for the door, slamming it for good measure, he leaves Connor with an early copy of the newspaper of record.

A FEW PARTING WORDS FROM THE EDITOR IN CHIEF

The next morning, the other Manolo drops.

"Connor? Please hold for Jillian Crowe."

I tell her I can't hold, but suddenly Jillian is on the line: "Whatever you did to alienate Chip Ralston and his people is one—"

"What *I* did to Chip Ralston? That son of a bitch is fucking my girlfriend."

"Well, tit for tat. You can hardly fault him for that, Connor. After your little adventure with his concubine. In fact I think that's very democratic of him. Droit du seigneur and all. But I'm afraid Lapidus has pulled eight pages of ads from the magazine."

"What?"

"Charles Lapidus—"

"Who, the wife beater?"

"And while there was no official explanation I think we both know who's to blame. You know, I kept thinking, you've been hanging out for long enough that by now you ought to be dry behind the ears. I kept waiting. At any rate, I don't think your heart was ever in this enterprise. I'm sure you'll find a position more worthy of your talents elsewhere. Your contract is up at the end of the year, yes? Please keep in mind that it's a small world we live in and any scurrilous allegations would pretty thoroughly sabotage your future prospects, limited as they might be. Well, I think that covers it. Goodbye Connor."

TWO WEEKS LATER, THEATER DISTRICT

Clustered around the side entrance of the Ed Sullivan Theater on West Fifty-third Street, home of *Late Night with David Letterman*, we are freezing our asses off, waiting for the stars. Two blue police barriers form a corridor from the curb, and a security guard hovers listlessly at the stage door. We press our crotches up against the barricades, autograph books and pens clutched to our chests, looking toward the street, stamping our cold feet for circulation. But we don't really mind the cold, which certifies our sincerity and our determination. (Besides which, some of us are just a *teeny* bit drunk.) The fair-weather fans are home on a day like this. The studio audience has already gone inside; while the standbys and the tourists are waiting at the front entrance. But these are amateurs, pallid enthusiasts, not like us. We're the real fans, the big fans. We are the biggest fans. As in "Hey, Clint, I'm your biggest fan."

Bearlike Clarence, for instance, with his huge, fur-hooded army-surplus parka, his scholarly thick black glasses, his ultra-professional mien, his unabashed air of a man engaged in an important pursuit at which he excels: "I just got Brooke Shields, man. She's a real nice lady. Real nice. Yeah, I got her over at NBC few minutes ago, she's on *Conan*. Not like that Geena Davis, man. Remember last week, she brush right past you, don't look at nobody, think she a fucking queen. Look like a drag queen, you ask me. Arnold, he's like that. Don't sign no autographs. Tell you who I like, I like Richard Harris. A gentleman, know what I'm saying? He be cool. Not like that Richard Chamberlain. Richard Chamberlain, he come through here he shake your hand, that sucks, man, what I'm gonna do with a handshake? Can't show your friends a handshake, you can't put it on your damn wall."

"Can't sell it," Charlie says, zipping up his Mets warm-up jacket. A plumber in Patchogue, Long Island, when he isn't here outside the Ed Sullivan Theater, or in the lobby of NBC headquarters in Rockefeller Center, he and his friend Tony are armed with unlined six-by-nine-inch index cards. They are fans, but their hero worship is tainted by mercenary motives. If they can get three cards signed, they will sell two to a dealer.

Clarence does not approve of Tony and Charlie. "I don't sell no autographs. I'm doing it for me, man, not like some of them. I ain't saying it's against the law, I'm just saying it don't reflect well on the rest of us, know what I'm saying? You got to have a certain respect for these people, right? Because they people too. You take the biggest superstar in the world, he's a person, same as you or me. Am I right? He got his life, he got his problems."

"Yeah," says Tony, "like, 'Gee, let's see, how often do I want my dick sucked today?'"

"Hey, fuck you, man. It's not all like that, you know what I'm saying?" Clarence speaks as if with the authority of one who has been a huge star in another, recent life, and who remembers it all too clearly. He addresses these remarks in part to the company at large and in part to his companion Vasya, whose blue eyes are foggy and slightly unfocused behind his thick glasses, the earflaps of his hunting cap askew, his chin spotted with lichenlike tufts of beard. Vasya carries an ancient Kodak Brownie camera which he holds up to his ear from time to time as if he expects it to say something.

Suddenly the throng goes taut and silent, congealing into a single quivering sensory organ, as a shiny black stretch fins up to the curb and stops, its cargo invisible behind the smoked glass. The uniformed driver marches officiously around the car to open the curbside door.

"Chip!" screams one of the photographers. "Over here!"

"Hey, Ralston!"

"I'm your biggest fan, Chip."

"How about an autograph, Chip?"

"Look over here! Smile!"

A CLOSE PERSONAL ENCOUNTER

The actor hesitates, framed in the open door of the limo, getting the lay of the land before launching himself toward the stage door, hunched, his head retracted as far as possible into the turtle shell of his jacket, moving quickly, but not quickly enough to dodge me as I slide under the police barrier and cut him off.

"Hey, Chip, I'm Connor McKnight." Savoring for a nanosecond the infusion of fear in his much admired and indeed very striking hazel eyes, I nail him with a headbutt aimed at the bridge of the nose which actually connects with his temple as he tries to duck away. Solid contact, nonetheless. Solid enough to hurt the shit out of my head.

"I'm your biggest fuckin' fan, Chip," I say.

He wobbles, clutching at the police barrier with one hand, his stunned skull with the other, then sinks to his knees just as the security guard tackles me and pins my face against the cold grainy concrete.

CONNOR FACES THE PRESS

After a couple of hours in the holding cell my name is called. Thankfully, the largest man in the cell, who'd just shot an associate of his over on Ninth Avenue, was no fan of Ralston's. When I announced the nature of my offense, he took me under his protection. Ralston had played cops in his last two outings and was pronounced to be a pussy.

Brooke is waiting for me out by the front desk. So is a reporter from the *Post*. A sallow man, ancient by tabloid standards—easily forty—he pushes back the bill of his NEW YORK IT AIN'T OVER cap and flips open his steno pad.

"Why'd you do it," he asks, as I finish signing out.

"I didn't like his acting choices."

"Is it true you've been stalking Chip Ralston for months?"

Brooke takes my arm and we bolt for the door. Outside, more reporters and photographers swarm up the steps.

"Connor, over here."

"Is that your girlfriend?"

"What's her name?"

"Hey, Connor."

"How about the two of you kissing for a picture?"

They pursue us as we race down the street. A reporter runs alongside of us, brandishing a tape recorder: "What about this rumor he owed you money on a drug deal?" Two paparazzi run up ahead of us and crouch down directly in our path on the sidewalk, clicking away.

"What rumor," asks Brooke.

"It becomes a rumor," I explain, "as soon as they quote you denying it. Just walk."

"Come on, Connor," says the reporter.

Incredibly, I can't help feeling strangely exhilarated by the attention of these men of the press and at the scrutiny of pedestrians. So this is what it's like, I think. My sordid little moment to shine. Not the limelight, exactly. More like the lemonlight, the reflected glory experienced by one-day sensations and the sexual partners of the stars. That yearning to exist, as they do, outside of themselves. Like Philomena, now. Brooke, however, is getting very upset.

After several blocks we duck into a Japanese restaurant. Japanese businessmen smoking at the bar. For a moment it's as if I've stepped back in time to Kyoto. Before Phil, before any of this.

To the reporter who follows us into the restaurant, I explain that Chip and I were lovers, that he had cruelly used and abused me. Which I figure should keep him busy for a while. Not to mention Chip's publicist. While he races back to the office I order up a gimlet.

"You can't keep drinking this way, Connor."

"You can't keep eating this way," I counter.

"I'm not eating."

"Precisely. You're anorexic, Brooke."

"*Me?* Are you out of your mind? I eat like a pig."

"Have you eaten today?"

"Sure, I've eaten."

"What?"

"I had some pretzels."

"You're sick, Brooke."

"And what are you?"

"I'm sad. I'm just incredibly fucking sad. Okay? Jesus. At least you haven't cut yourself recently."

"Please don't yell at me. I just really need you not to be critical right now, all right?"

"Okay." I take her hand, her thin, bony hand, until she pulls it away to light a new cigarette from the glowing butt of the old one.

"Are you missing her?" Brooke asks.

"What do you think?"

"Do you suppose," she asks, "you would've married Philomena if not for me?"

"What would you have to do with it?"

"I don't know—you feeling like you needed to take care of

me?" Before I can think of how to respond, she adds, "I guess that's pretty self-aggrandizing."

"Unfortunately, I can't really blame anybody but myself. Would you eat a California roll if I ordered one?"

RITES OF THE SEASON

"So," Brooke says as we step into the limpid gloom of the midtown canyon, "what would you like to do? Go to Rockefeller Center, see the tree and watch the skaters?"

For some reason I find this hilarious. A boy and his sister taking in the sights. I'm laughing so hard I have to hug Brooke for support.

"Then maybe check out the windows at Saks, catch the Christmas show at Radio City?"

She's laughing, too, patting my back.

"I don't know if they let felons in to see the Rockettes."

"What do we care? Back home there's oranges hanging on the trees. Can these fucking New Yorkers say that? You realize we're leaving tomorrow?"

"It's not going to be Christmas without Corvetta," Brooke says, her smile disappearing. Then under the influence of a new inspiration, she smiles. "I know, let's not go home. Let's go to the Bahamas. Get away from all these white people with their shopping bags and their family curses."

"We can't get away from them. We *are* them."

Seeing the sadness in her face, I hold her in my arms, the pedestrian traffic of Fifth Avenue surging around us. Me thinking of Philomena standing on a stool like an angel in a white robe, putting the star on the Christmas tree last year.

REVENGE FANTASIES

—Chip Ralston, gored by an elk in the hills outside Livingston, Montana. In the groin.

—Philomena betrayed by Chip, who runs off with Milla Jovovich. Major tabloid coverage of their Las Vegas wedding.

—Chip dying of a drug overdose on the sidewalk outside the Viper Room in Los Angeles as passersby pass by. Later, in the parking lot actress Christina Applegate mimics his spastic death throes for the amusement of her friends.

—Philomena, diagnosed with terminal illness, comes home to New York. Connor McKnight—a true, if agnostic, Christian—takes her back, against the advice of friends and family, and nurses her through her long illness. Her dying words: "Oh, Connor, I'm so sorry. You were the only man I ever loved."

PAJAMA PARTY

Understanding that I'm not eager to go back alone to my apartment, Brooke invites me to spend the night before we fly home. She agrees to eat if I agree not to drink—a difficult trade for both of us. Corvetta calls from the airport to say her flight was delayed, that she's going straight to her hotel and she'll see us after her meeting tomorrow. I'm just as happy to have the night alone with Brooke. When the food arrives she picks at the Szechuan vegetables, wielding the chopsticks like a jeweler, deconstructing emerald peapods, examining water chestnuts for color and clarity.

Brooke's in her pajamas—actually an old pair of Dad's flannels from, you guessed it, Brooks Brothers. "It's like when you were little," she says happily. "And you'd sneak into my room."

"Before you went away to school," I say, my voice betraying a resentment which catches even me by surprise.

Though she got straight A's in the "honors" program at the local high school, it was finally decided, after she'd been caught smoking pot in her bedroom, that Brooke needed to be finished at boarding school. While Mom and Dad tripped over themselves and tossed back an extra glass every day attempting to *avoid* knowing what she might be up to, my sister was finally caught in the act by Daisy, our fierce Baptist housekeeper of many years, who is a far more compelling authority figure than either of our parents, with much stricter notions of how a white girl from a good family should comport herself. Daisy made such a fuss on this occasion that my father was embarrassed into action. Brooke was resigned, as I recall, but I was devastated. And I was angry at her because it almost seemed as if she wanted to get caught; she knew Daisy was in the house, and Daisy's movements are never discreet, her advent inevitably presaged by huffing and puffing and a trembling of furniture.

"You ruined my childhood," I say, "all because you had to smoke a joint in the house."

"It wasn't pot," Brooke says.

"What do you mean it wasn't pot?"

"I was caught with Sandy what's-his-name, the housepainter. You knew that."

"I didn't know that."

"I think it was more a case of you didn't want to know it."

CONNOR McKNIGHT, TAXIDERMIST

"You were a funny kid," Brooke says as she strokes my hair. "We were so isolated out there in the groves and I was afraid you'd turn out really weird. Collecting stamps and coins and beetles and playing with lizards. Oh, my God! Remember your taxidermy phase? I'd almost forgotten that. When Vermeer the Parrot died and you decided to stuff him? You never were very good at letting go of things, now that I think about it. Dad took you to the taxidermist in town. And you started that correspondence course. All those peckerwoods coming to the back door with poached game and roadkill? I'd open up the freezer looking for a Creamsicle and there'd be a dead owl staring out at me. I think that was when I stopped eating on a regular basis."

CHIP RALSTON, PLUCKY
CRIME VICTIM

At eleven-thirty we watch *Letterman*, the very show that was taped only hours ago, in spite of an incident which host and guest thrillingly recount for the audience. Ralston's a big hit, carrying an ice pack, explaining how the martial-arts training for his new picture had come in handy when fending off his attacker—the crazed stalker—and commiserating with Dave about the way in which well-deserved adulation occasionally, in the case of a few warped individuals, modulates to dangerous obsession. "But, hey, Dave, it goes with the territory, doing what we do, being in the public eye, and I'm definitely not going to let an isolated incident like this cut me off from my fans or make me paranoid. Hell, this is the greatest job in the world, and you've got to take the rough with the smooth."

The studio audience roars its approval.

FURTHER REVENGE SCENARIOS

—Connor McKnight as Toshiro Mifune, in the movie *Yojimbo*, wrapped in ratty kimono, sword thrust in his obi, striding bandy-legged down a dusty street in a rural Japanese village. The burg eerily silent. Suddenly, men pour out of the buildings on either side of the street, swords raised. They rush McKnight, who slices them down one by one, until only their leader, evil Yakuza chieftain Chip Ralston, remains standing. Terrified, Ralston tries to run, and then, finding himself in a dead-end alley, pulls a gun from his kimono and fires it—a dastardly violation of Bushido, the samurai martial code. Grazed by the shot, McKnight advances fearlessly, to cut the coward down. McKnight sheaths his sword and strides down the street to the brothel, where he throws aside the mama-san like a sack of grain and tells the courtesan Philomena-chan that she is free. "Take me with you," she pleads, clutching his knees. "I travel alone," he responds, shaking himself free and striding off with stoic, bandy-legged nobility down the dusty street.

—Chip Ralston performing dinner theater in Winter Haven, Florida, his last five movies having bombed, numbers four and five going directly to video without benefit of theatrical release. Connor McKnight, visiting his ancestral home with his beautiful wife, actress/model Milla Jovovich, takes his grateful aging parents out for an entertaining dinner before flying off the next day to the Caribbean on his private jet. After the show, Connor graciously sends a drink to the former star, along with his card, no address or title—just his name engraved in Antique Shaded Roman on Crane's ecru notecard stock; on the back of this card Connor has written down two telephone numbers, one the extension of a junior agent at William Morris, the other the toll-free telephone number of the Hair Club of America, with the notation "Word to the Wise."

THAT'S ME IN THE SPOTLIGHT

The next morning I wake up in Brooke's bed, alone. I can hear her moving around in the next room. It's almost noon. Without moving from the bed I check my answering service. Sixteen messages—including interview requests from New York and national tabloids, as well as *Hard Copy* and *A Current Affair*. Also a call from a casting director who says she saw my picture and would like me to read for a part in a movie that starts shooting next week.

Erasing all of the messages, I crawl out of Brooke's bed, and walk softly to the door.

SCENE FROM AN IMAGINARY SCREENPLAY

CLOSE UP ON *the edge of a razor blade which seems to be floating in space.*

Still CLOSE, *but drawing back we see that the blade is attached to a retractable paint scraper which is held by a feminine hand.*

REVERSE ANGLE ON

CONNOR MCKNIGHT, *standing framed in the doorway of the bedroom, looking on in horror.*

REVERSE ON

BROOKE MCKNIGHT, *a very pretty if somewhat haggard woman of thirty-five, whose hand is holding the paint scraper, staring at it intently.*

ANOTHER ANGLE *from which we see several scars on the inside of Brooke's bare left arm.*

CONNOR (offscreen)

Brooke!

She continues to stare at the blade, as if in a trance. . . .

D E C O R A T I N G

Connor approaches cautiously, as she continues to stare at the dangerous tool in her hand. He kisses her cheek as he pries her fingers from the instrument. Which seems to break the spell.

"Good morning," she says brightly. Her hands suddenly free, she fishes for a cigarette. Now Connor notices that she's wearing a paint-spattered smock. Half a dozen cans of paint, lids removed, stand on a fan of newspaper; all of the books in her bookshelf are stacked on the floor. The wall beside the fireplace is mottled with peach- and salmon-colored splotches, any one of which, on a normal day, might nicely complement her own carroty complexion.

"Did I by any chance lend you my old paperback of Jim Harrison's *Legends of the Fall?* Remember that cover? I can't find it anywhere, it had that nice Santa Fe salmon kind of shade in the background, I really think that would be just a great color in here, don't you?"

"Brooke, what's with this sudden interest in interior decor? We're supposed to be going home for Christmas in three hours."

The smell of paint makes Connor nervous, signifying fresh starts and bright expectations. He watches his sister virtually spin around the room, pausing here and there to move a chair or tap the ash from her cigarette.

"I was going through my drawers and I found this apricot-colored pullover Mom gave me a few years ago from Lands' End, then I thought about how depressing these walls were. They look like the walls of some incredibly dreary municipal office in some dying rust belt town. I mean, they're not even white for God's sake, they're the color of smog or something—like the air on a depressing day in Los Angeles." She scrutinizes the paint splotches on the wall. "Which one do you honestly like the best?"

She asks this exactly as if Connor were very well known for being cagey about revealing his favorite color.

"Brooke, can you hear me?" Having seen this dervishing behavior before, he backs her against the wall, puts his arms around her and squeezes gently. "We're leaving today. Corvetta should be here anytime."

"I kind of like the smoky peach—of course I can hear you—but it's hard to tell from just a little dab of it, when you do the whole room it might be way too dark."

Connor increases the pressure of his embrace, crushing his face into the coppery mass of her coconut-shampoo-and-cigarette-scented hair. With his cheek pressed against her neck he registers her monologue as a series of distant vibrations. Suddenly it seems very peaceful here, within the thicket of her semifragrant hair, an unexpected ambience of sanctuary reminiscent of childhood. As Brooke buzzes on, Connor could almost fall asleep. But she won't let him, becoming shrill in her defense of the ocher family of colors. He squeezes almost as hard as he can, until she finally stops babbling.

"We're going home, Brooke."

"Jerry's getting married again," she says in a tiny voice.

"When did you hear this?"

"This morning. He called to tell me so I wouldn't have to read about it in the press, as he so self-aggrandizingly put it. Not so that I wouldn't *hear* about it, which would have been a more than adequate locution. So that I wouldn't *have to read about it in the press.*" She pauses to consume half a Marlboro in a single breath. "Like it'll make the cover of fucking *People* next week. Shit, it probably will. He's getting married on the beach in Bali. One of his students—surprise, surprise. I said, 'Jerry, I really don't think it behooves a scientist to be quite so predictable, so transparently and simplistically *determined* an entity.'"

"Do you still love him?"

She sighs and considers. "No. If I really loved him I'd want him to be happy, wouldn't I?"

Well, Connor thinks, this would seem to go a long way toward explaining the painting and the color chart and the razor blade.

"Look, if you promise to pack, I promise to help you paint when we get back."

It's not as if he's so eager to go home for the holidays. For the last few years Philomena had redeemed the tired rituals of Christmas with her bright childish expectations. Their first year in Japan she found a tiny bonsai tree and pinned stockings to the wall above the kerosene heater, and between this recollection and the sight of Brooke in her manic state it's all he can do to keep from taking the paint scraper to his own wrists.

THE SPOTLIGHT, CONT.

The flight leaves at four. Fearful of leaving Brooke alone, I convince her to come to my apartment and help me pack, more or less on the pretext that I'm afraid to be alone in the place. Which is more or less true. Fortunately Corvetta calls from her meeting; I tell her to meet us there.

We stop at the newsstand. A picture of yours truly on page 3 of the *Post* this morning, very soigné in my Patagonia ski jacket, pinned on the sidewalk beneath the security guard outside the theater, my expression that of the dazed psychopath. I recognize Vasya's calf-high vulcanized rubber boots in the background—a veridical detail which is more realistic and familiar to me than my own face, or the written account of the incident. KARATE KID CHOPS CHIP. The *Post* reporter somehow uncovered my Japan background and apparently concluded that I was a Karate Kung Fu Aikido adept, black belt in half a dozen deadly arts. The karate notion synergizes neatly with the promotion of Chip's latest flick, which has a ninja subplot. An unnamed spokesman reports that I had made numerous threatening phone calls to Chip's unlisted number which I presumably obtained in my role as a former celebrity correspondent for *CiaoBella!* and categorically denies that there was ever any romantic relationship between myself and the star. A spokesman for *CiaoBella!* citing "erratic behavior" chimes in that my contract is about to expire. An "associate" at the magazine confirms that I am "kind of a loner, a bit of a weirdo." Riding downtown, I pass the tabloids to Brooke and flip through *Beau Monde*, where I discover Kevin Shipley's review of *Walled-In*.

> At least Peter Benchley had the courage of his lowbrow convictions when he decided to rewrite Moby Dick. [*No, actually, but I saw the movie.*] The same cannot be said for Jeremy Green, the Brad Pitt of the Upper West Side lit set. After slogging through "Walled-In," Green's unspeakably pretentious homage to Thoreau, as in Henry David, I am bracing myself for Jay McInerney's take on *Leaves of Grass*.

I can't honestly say whether I would have read on or closed the magazine at that moment out of respect for my erstwhile friend, but in any case the cab pulled up in front of my apartment as I finished the first paragraph.

In New York City, particularly in the Village, it is not unusual to find people camped out on your stoop. Of the young woman sitting on my step I remember registering a purely visual sensation—that my landlady's Christmas wreath seemed from my vantage to form a green halo behind the springy mass of her dark hair. I placed a solicitous arm around my sister's shoulder as she stepped out of the cab.

When the stoop sitter stood up I assumed she was making way for us. Pretty, I thought, noting a resemblance to the actress Jennifer Lopez. She started down the steps, staring at me intently, as if she knew me. A cab shuddered to a stop beside us. Turning, I saw Corvetta climbing from the back, an expression of puzzlement crossing her face, as if *she* didn't recognize us after all. I followed her gaze, turning back in time to see the girl in the leather jacket raise her arm and hold it aloft, her curious stance—and perhaps the afterimage of the spiky crown of wreath—putting me in mind of Lady Liberty, clutching in her hand something which in the winter sunlight glittered like a tiny torch. . . .

ONE YEAR LATER

To: Scribbler
From: Philo
Subject:
Dear Connor:
I feel like so much has happened, I don't really know where to begin. I wanted to write you after I heard about Jeremy but I didn't really think it was my place. God, it was such a shock. Coming so soon after I left it must have been pretty devastating. I wish I had handled it better. But it sounds like you have made the most of adversity. I heard you were staying at the Chateau Marmont a few months ago, but I thought the last thing you would want is to hear from me. But if you feel like it, it would be nice to see you the next time you come out to L.A. But I will understand if you don't.
Love, Phil

CONCORD OUT OF DISCORD

December is the perfect month for a Florida wedding, warm evenings scented with orange blossoms—that strange moment when one crop is on the tree and another is blossoming beside it. Although in this case the epithalamia are tinged with melancholy, since Dad has been forced to sell the old homestead after mortgaging it to the hilt. But here we are, gathered beneath a tent beside the old white house, with its porches and gables, the groves spreading around us in orderly fecundity. Upstairs, the relics of my childhood—the taxidermied animals and juvenile poetry, the stamp collection, Marvel comics, baseball cards, certificates of merit and love letters—are packed in boxes for shipment to New York. In a few weeks a family from Ohio will try its luck here. Dad has been off the sauce for three months now, so chances are good that the ceremony will go off without any embarrassing incidents. My parents have bought a little condo just off the beach in Naples and with luck will have enough cash to last them. If not, Dr. Doug has pledged to help out. After all, he's family now. Despite my worst intentions I find it harder and harder to dislike him. I felt terrible when he asked me to be his best man. In fact, I'm about to deliver a toast to the groom. Among the sentiments I hope to express is my belief I'm at best the second best man, as Brooke told me over a year ago in New York.

Brooke is—dare I say it—happy, and that's miracle enough for me just now, unlikely as it has seemed for so many years. She has convinced Doug to take a year off from his practice to work with refugees in central Africa, where she will accompany him as a nurse's aide. Since last Christmas she's gained ten pounds; soon she'll be almost hefty enough to sign with the Ford Agency. A beautiful bride, crooked ear and all. I'm put in mind of that quaint nineteenth-century medical treatment—bleeding the patient. It's as if, having dabbled at mutilating herself all those years, getting well and truly cut by a frenzied girl with a boxcutter seems to have removed the old ill humors. Her parotid gland may require further scrutiny, but the truth is she's perversely pleased, given her lifelong distrust of pulchritude, to sport a slight disfigurement: a raised pink crescent below her earlobe. Fortunately, she turned away at just the right moment.

At Brooke's insistence, her assailant, Jennie Rodriguez, is a guest at the wedding; her doctor felt her attendance would provide a sense of closure to the unfortunate episode. On two occasions I have participated in her court-ordered therapy, which has been successful at least to the extent of convincing her that slashing people with boxcutters is socially unacceptable, even under the influence of peer pressure. She's actually a very sweet girl. She feels particularly terrible that she attacked the wrong woman—my sister instead of my girlfriend. "Isn't it weird," she said just a moment ago, "the way it all turned out."

"Isn't it," I agreed.

Jennie loves Florida, at least what she has seen of it, and tells me she's thinking of moving to Miami.

Bob Jamison, of Flemington, New Jersey, remains free on bail, and seems, on the basis of his lawyer's statements to the press, to believe that he acted well within the rights of a homeowner when he shot an intruder in his kitchen at 3 a.m. The shooting occurred the night before *Beau Monde* hit the newsstands. Although some have suggested a link, it seems unlikely that Jeremy could have seen Kevin Shipley's review before he decided to drive to New Jersey in the middle of the night in order to liberate his dog; no copy was found in his possession. Subsequent reviews—and there were a lot of them, posthumously—were almost universally laudatory. *Time's* reviewer found premonitions of early demise in both of the books, while another portrayed his death as the tragic surrender of a soul too delicate to survive the malicious and ill-informed judgment of a glib and inhospitable critical establishment. I think Jeremy would have been particularly pleased to see the word *glib* in that context. I was pleased when the *New York Post's* page 6 reported that Kevin and Jeremy were rivals for the affections of Tina Christian. On the other hand, if his employers found this news disturbing, they have so far kept their chagrin to themselves.

As for me, I have a small scar on the palm of my hand where I grabbed at the boxcutter a year ago, which I cherish as the emblem of larger wounds. For months, my first conscious sensation on waking in the morning was the dull ache of loss, complicated almost immediately by feelings of guilt, as if I had to choose between mourning Jeremy and missing Phil—as if I was afraid that some genie would suddenly appear to offer me the choice of bringing back one or the other.

I managed to avoid seeing Chip Ralston's latest movie, in which Philomena had a small part. (I did catch Jason Townes's new flick—and was mildly surprised to see my old friend Pallas appear briefly on-screen.) I'm not unhappy to report that Chip's movie opened poorly and raced to video. According to *People* magazine, he's still dating Phil, though she has her own apartment. According to starzzz, an Internet gossip page, he's stepping out with a stripper, and Phil's recent communication leads me to credit the latter report. Every day for a year I checked my e-mail and my answering machine with the conscious if dwindling hope that I would hear from her. I shrieked with delight when the letter finally appeared on my screen, but I have not yet responded. The heart has its reasons, but they are seldom reasonable. If the concept of romantic love has any use, it is to denote that vast residue of inexplicable attraction which is not covered under the categories of blind lust and well-informed self-interest.

As soon as I finish the first draft of my screenplay—probably the *day* I finish—I am going to see her. But not until then. I'm waiting because I want to go to her in my moment of triumph. And because—could it be?—I'm afraid our actual reunion may be less shapely and conclusive than the version I am conjuring for the screen.

HOW CONNOR GOT HIS START IN SHOWBIZ

In his will Jeremy named me his literary executor. It's a busy side-line, working with Rachel, his agent: requests for serial rights, reprint rights, movie options, translations. After all the lurid publicity, *Walled-In* sold briskly in hardcover and is about to be released in paperback. People for the Ethical Treatment of Animals—the sole beneficiary of his estate—stands to collect a handsome annuity for some years to come.

If I felt awkward about using my position as Jeremy's executor to champion my own cause as screenwriter, in the end I reasoned: Who better than me? The studio was amenable, partly on the basis of the screenplay I pulled out of my drawer, partly because it could hire me for scale—a negligible sum in its scheme of things. I'm currently adapting his story "Model Behavior," which was optioned by Fox. Someone who works at Brad Pitt's production company is said to have given him a copy of the book; based on his expression of interest, Rachel and I were able to make a respectable deal for the underlying rights as well as my first draft plus polish with an optional second draft on the screenplay. Brad's a long shot, of course; at our last production meeting, Chip Ralston was one of the names that came up. After pretending to consider this option, I said I didn't really think he was right for the part. At the moment the producers are pretending to be interested in my opinion.

ANOTHER HAPPY ENDING

We're pitching it as "a noirish romantic comedy," the story of a tormented writer's brief and tempestuous affair with his best friend's model fiancée. It's been impossible, of course, to remain entirely faithful to Jeremy's story, film and literature being different media, after all. But I comfort myself with the knowledge that infidelity is precisely the subject of Jeremy's story. In our early discussions the producer told me we needed a third act, and at the moment we all seem to be, as he put it recently, "on the same page."

It's weird, working on the third and final act, the part that wasn't in Jeremy's story. The part beyond this. But the final scene is already written. It wrote itself, as they say. I mean, there was never any question about the ending. That's one thing you can say for the movies.

In the end she comes back to me.

"Jay McInerney has proven himself not only
a brilliant stylist but a master of characterization, with
a keen eye for incongruities of urban life."
—*The New York Times Book Review*

BRIGHT LIGHTS, BIG CITY

Living in Manhattan as if he owned it, a young man tries to
outstrip mortality and the recurring approach of dawn with
nothing but good will, controlled substances and the wit to
sustain him. Jay McInerney's first novel is a pitch-perfect
rendition of the urban angst and party frenzy of the 1980s.

Fiction/0-394-72641-3

BRIGHTNESS FALLS

In this elegy for New York in the 1980s, McInerney maps
the fault lines spreading through the once impenetrable
marriage of Russell and Corrine Calloway and chronicles
Russell's wild scheme to seize control of the publishing
house at which he works.

Fiction/0-679-74532-7

LAST OF THE SAVAGES

This chronicle of a generation, as enacted by two men who
represent all the passions and extremes of the class of 1969,
is the story of Patrick Keane and Will Savage. Despite their
different backgrounds, the two remain friends for over thirty years even as they pursue radically divergent destinies.

Fiction/Literature/0-679-74952-7

RANSOM

A young American trying to become a karate master in Kyoto, the ancient capital of Japan, Christopher Ransom seeks a purity and simplicity he could not find in the U.S. But he is unable to exorcize the terrors of violence, death, and betrayal he encountered both in his earlier travels to the Khyber Pass and, now, facing an implacable enemy in Japan.

Fiction/0-394-74118-8

STORY OF MY LIFE

Alison Poole is a twenty-year-old actress already well versed in the fast paced life of clubs, sex, money and power in New York City. As she races toward an emotional breakdown, McInerney gives us a hilarious yet oddly touching portrait of a postmodern Holly Golightly coming to terms with a world in which everything is permitted and nothing really matters.

Fiction/0-679-72257-2